GH01043786

IT PAYS THE MORTGAGE

by Paula T Griffiths

FOR DAD

Who never went to the pub straight from work but came home to be with us.

Who, when working away, packed his job in and came home when I wrote him a letter asking, "Don't you love us anymore?"

Who drove us around in his car "sight-seeing" to Bidston Hill and New Brighton, while our mum worked an evening shift at Cadburys to earn extra pennies.

Who entertained us on his piano accordion when the weather was too bad to go out, and the sound of which still brings memories and tears flooding back whenever I hear one.

Who was broken-hearted when I rowed with him and fed him deaf and dumb butties for a fortnight and mum had to negotiate a peace deal.

Who was always there for us.

PREFACE

Silvia Fernsby was always searching for answers. Sometimes to questions she hadn't even asked herself yet. Her struggle to understand her own mental abilities as well as those of her superiors was often daunting, but Silvia battled on - regardless of fate producing that recurring sensation of wading through treacle. You can walk towards the moon but it never gets any closer.

She wanted to establish herself as a career woman - but in which direction she didn't know. She'd reached a crossroads so many times, usually after fighting off the competition, who thought they knew better because they had university degrees but actually didn't know a lot - SILVIA HAD THE EXPERIENCE – and a certificate from MENSA saying she had an IQ of 137, which meant she was in the top 6% of the population.

Yet, here she was again standing on the precipice of jacking it all in – similar to a demented lemming about to throw herself off the edge of the cliff but not wanting the buggers to win.

So each time she doubted herself she took the route of knowledge to prove to herself that she knew as much as they did - if not more; that she COULD grasp an idea and follow it through, but every time she was beaten back by the same system that let these bozos cross her path, step over her head and carry on up the ladder of fame and fortune.

And she had a black belt in Feng Shui…

A resume of all the crap jobs you have to do and the crap you have to take, because It Pays The Mortgage.
All names have been changed to protect the innocent and the guilty.

DECISIONS, DECISIONS

Silvia Fernsby aspired to be a businesswoman but it didn't help
matters when she discovered everyone around her was as thick as
two short planks. She hadn't exactly struggled through school and was
always at the top of her section – one of the top five out of a class of
40 pupils – they had bigger classes back in 1968. But she wasn't like
all the other brain boxes – serious, dull and with charisma bypasses.
They didn't understand her cheeky sense of humour and so she was
always in trouble with her mentors because of it.

At the age of 12 her Father enquired as to what career she was going
to forge for herself. Not particularly interested in anything at that time
she informed him of her indecision, "Dunno," which prompted the
ranting reply of a man incensed by her indifference and who was
obviously trying to keep up with the Jones's and impress the Masons
group he belonged to.
"Terry Sole's daughter wants to be a teacher!" he shouted at her in
frustration.
Terry Sole was a close friend of her Father and his daughter was 14.
"Well, when I'm 14 maybe I'll know what I want to be, so ask me again
then," Silvia replied.

He stormed off with a bright red face, about to explode with anger.
It wasn't exactly Silvia's fault. In those days schools never informed
the pupils as to what was on offer work wise within their communities,
let alone further afield. Most of the boys did wood and metalwork and
got a job in Cammell Laird or drove the local buses and the women
worked in factories like Cadburys or the corner shop. It was assumed
that you would learn to pass the 11-plus exam and go onto High
School, where they would mould you into taking secretarial work or
perhaps nursing (SRN or SEN) and if you failed you went to Middle

School and got positions in the local telephone exchange (GPO) dishing out peoples telephone numbers from directory enquiries.

As Silvia was nearly always at the top of her class, she was taken out of her classroom one day and lead into the assembly hall. She had no idea why until she saw rows of desks and children waiting to take an exam – the 11-plus. Teachers never discussed important things with pupils back then, they just did what they thought was right. Unfortunately, there were no spare desks available and so they returned her to the classroom again, nonplussed, so to speak. No consultation with her parents that she might be a bright child and need to pursue this had ever taken place, so they were none the wiser either.

So off to Middle School she went, along with all her friends, for two years because then, the government of the day decided that education needed a reshuffle and the High School was to be abolished with the introduction of Comprehensives – to give everyone a fairer chance they implied – with all pupils going to Middle School, then onto a Comprehensive for the last two years of general schooling. It was then up to the pupil if they wanted to stay on till Sixth Form and carry on their education or leave to get a job.

At 14 Silvia still didn't know what she wanted to do. Her school introduced a secretarial curriculum so she thought she'd have a go. "How difficult could it be?" she asked her friend Mona, "I used to practice on my Junior Petite typewriter when I was bored on a Sunday."

All the other kids spent their Sundays down the outdoor pool on Harrison Drive but Silvia couldn't swim so was never asked along. "That was the highlight of my Sunday," she informed Mona, "that and then trying to record the Top 20 at 6pm on my cassette player because we couldn't afford to buy the records."

Mona nodded in agreement.

To take three examinations in shorthand, typing and commerce she had to give up four subjects: Geography – the teacher had a nervous breakdown; History – the teacher thought the world was flat; Chemistry – the Prof. would throw the board rubber at anyone caught talking in class and make them remove their nail polish with pure acetone from the locked cupboard; Biology – embarrassing diagrams of people's private parts (and how ugly they were too!) and the thought of cutting up small creatures of nature was enough to make her sick. Once Silvia realised she'd never have the stomach to make a brain surgeon - too much gooey mess - it was an easy call, she joined the secretarial team.

Silvia excelled. Her typing skills soon notched up to 60 words a minute, she could take dictation from the News at 10 and the world of commerce was a synch. Then just when things were going great, fate dealt a terrible blow. Her teacher fell down the steps of the school annexe and died from a blot clot on the leg.

An Irish locum took over and Silvia struggled to understand anything she said.
"Now girls, diddly diddly diddly diddly, on page 5," she'd tell them. Silvia would look at her with a blank expression on her face and quickly look to see what everyone else was turning to. It could have been French for all she knew, she'd only ever been used to hearing a watered down version of scouse coming from the Wirral.

Mrs. Diddly could never remember where they were up to from one week to the next and on several occasions repeated previous lessons. "All she needs to do is write the bloody page number down for each class," she muttered to Belinda, who had taken the classes with her, but they never seemed to get past Hire Purchase Agreements and who was Silvia to remind her - she'd only get into trouble for being cheeky. Her grades began to suffer and fell below the national average as she lost interest in all but the typing - you didn't have to understand anyone to be good at typing as it was all practised from a book.

Two years later, when the school bell rang for the final time at 3.30pm for the summer break, Silvia was out of the school gates like a shot. She vaguely heard the Head Mistress enquiring something about those wishing to return in September to join the 6th form. Silvia never went back.

SATURDAY JOB

Silvia had taken a Saturday job with her friend Belinda in the back room of a bakery where they were informed that they could eat all the cakes they wanted - and they did. From 9am – 1pm they rolled pastry for the pies, inserting a dollop into a pastry case on a moulding machine. Plunging down the handle, the hotplate descended onto the ball of dough and spread it perfectly into the silver foil case making the outer shell of the pie ready for the filling - meat and potato, mince and gravy or pork and jelly.

They cleaned out the baking bowls, scrubbed the galvanized baking trays in the yard and occasionally hosed down the two trainee master bakers at the same time. They'd pretend they were Sergeant Schultz from Hogan's Heroes by placing huge mixing bowls on their heads and scoff hordes of glace cherries from huge plastic Tupperware bowls. Their jobs had quickly grown to a few extra hours on the way home from school a couple of nights a week making cake mixes for the next day's baking. It was her best friend Belinda's Auntie's cake shop in the local village and the residents used to queue for the bread, fresh out of the oven. Silvia and Belinda earned £3 a week and got paid their princely sum on a Saturday after their shift - just enough to buy a train ticket over to Liverpool and a David Bowie LP for £1.50

and have some left over for a pot of blue eye shadow, the return fare, and a bottle of pop to go out that night to the Cap disco.

One morning, bleary-eyed, Silvia saw a small creature dart across the kitchen floor at the back of the bakery.

"Oh, look, a mouse!" she shouted excitedly.

"Shhhhhh," came the reply back, as a hand was clasped over her mouth and the door to the bakery shop slammed shut. 'Don't let the customers hear you," the Auntie hushed back and pushed her out into the yard.

Silvia continued to hose down the concrete and waited for Belinda to finish serving in the shop and the two of them opened the cooling oven door and popped their wet shoes in there to dry off, helped themselves to a fresh loaf and cut two thick slices, popped them in the toaster and smothered them in butter and jam from the 28 pound tins stacked around the bakery, bliss after a hard morning on their feet.

Belinda had a liking for fresh cream cakes and trifles and hated synthetic cream, but her Auntie could never tell the difference and used to get Belinda to test the bowls she'd whisked up whilst making the Victoria sponges and frangipane cakes - it might have brought in complaints from customers if they had been sold a fresh cream cake only to discover it was synthetic!

"Yuk! That one's synthetic," Belinda would inform her Auntie, spitting it out.

Silvia on the other hand favoured the sweet marzipan that was glued onto a shortbread biscuit with apricot jam and covered in icing.

"Yummy, now that's what I call a sugar-buzz!" she'd smile cheekily.

One day they went AWOL with a couple of egg custards and hid in the cloakroom. It was dark so they couldn't see what they were eating. They could hear Auntie enquiring as to their whereabouts outside in the kitchen. As they bit into the pastries their mouths were met with a lumpy, congealed mess. "Eghhhh!" Auntie could hear a noise, she walked over to the cloakroom door and opened it to find the two of them in there covered in the egg custard they had spat out, because it hadn't been stirred enough to set properly the night before.

Those were the days when work was fun and innocent.

INTO THE LION'S DEN

And so it was that Silvia left school in 1974 at the tender age of sixteen and with a few CSE's tucked under her slender belt. With only a grade 3 in English her peers said she'd never make an author. In those days, women were advised to become secretaries or shop assistants to earn their living, especially if you lived on a council estate like Silvia and her friends did, it seemed there was little choice for you. Silvia's friend Mona was horrified!

"I haven't studied for 'O' levels (she was brainy) to become a shop assistant!" she shouted at the Career's Adviser, promptly shoved back her chair and stormed out of the room in three-inch high platform heels at the end of her spindly legs. Silvia and Mona contemplated each other.

"We could open a boutique and call it 'Size 10'," Mona suggested.

They both had a keen interest in sewing and often used an old electric sewing machine - circa 1950 - to create their seasonal wardrobes, the pedal of which would often become stuck at strategic points in the sewing process forcing one of them to dive under the table to free it, whilst the other skilfully manipulated any sharp bends the dressmaker's pattern would be steering her into whilst racing along at 60 miles an hour! They both became secretaries.

After 6 weeks job hunting, 10 job applications and two interviews for junior positions she was almost destined to return to the Stalag ex-High School, but fate decided that was not the way to go and gave her a lovely job in an insurance company in Liverpool. "The Totally Boring Insurance Company" to be exact.

Silvia went out that night to celebrate with Mona, they had a great night at the local disco, the Chelsea Reach, and they danced all night and had two sweet Martini's with lemonade. On a loo break for a breather they reapplied their lipstick in the mirrors and checked their hair was still in place and that their mascara hadn't run down their faces with the condensation and sweat.

The Ladies was always great for overhearing conversations from disgruntled girlfriends moaning about their boyfriends and the antics they got up to.
"Do you know what that git said to me last night," they'd enlighten their friend, "the swine wants to go on holiday with his friends, and not me, wants me to lose weight, put on weight, wear less makeup, wear more makeup, move in with him, move out." Delete as applicable.
"I said to her and she said to me," they both laughed in unison as they walked out, back onto the dance floor.

On their way out to get a taxi a boy jumped in front of her wearing a big beaming smile and said, "Hi". It was Hock, Mr. Seriously Handsome But Troubled, a Barry Manilow look-alike.

It was a face she recognised, that of an old flame and she hadn't seen him for over 12 months, since she'd been away on holiday with Belinda to a holiday camp in Wales and when she got back he'd met someone else.

She didn't notice at first but her friend noticed the love bite on his neck. She was heartbroken; he was her first true love. But here he was now kissing her and promising to call the following night when she got home from work.

Silvia remembered the first time they were together. She was fifteen when she started going to the youth club, "The Cap" in an old converted cinema the Capitol. It wasn't love at first sight; in fact she didn't notice him at all at first, she was more interested in dancing. It was only when Mona started seeing one of his friends that she spotted the three other lads with him all dressed in smart suits. They all went by nicknames and were a lot older at 20, and all had jobs. Mona and Silvia had been in their last year of school.

Hock was cheeky in his approach and it made Silvia laugh. Although not desperately attractive, he had a certain charisma. He asked Silvia if she would like to accompany him for a growler and a cup of splog. Roughly translated this turned out to be no more than a meat pie and a cup of tea. But the frowning look Silvia gave him, like he was speaking a foreign language she didn't understand, was enough to get him interested.

They went to Chester Zoo for their first date and they arranged to meet up the following night and the following day and everyday after that, they became inseparable. Even his Father used to save up his copper coins so Hock always had change to call her from the phone box at the top of his road.

One night, at the cinema, just as the film was about to start, he turned toward Silvia and whispered that he loved her. She was gob-smacked. No one had ever told her that they loved her before - not even her parents, even though they did - and she was so stunned that she didn't know what to say. Of course, she felt the same but couldn't get the words out, so she said nothing.

Hock was upset. He had confessed his undying love for her and Silvia hadn't verbally returned his affections as he had expected her to. Silvia remained a mystery to Hock for the next three years. She reckoned that's what kept him interested for so long - he couldn't really fathom her out. But there was nothing to fathom, she was just naïve. Silvia was now seeing him six nights a week, because Thursdays was girl's night down at the Chelsea and she'd never give up her friends for a man!

Silvia liked the simple things in life and liked life to be simple. Hock was always trying to unravel things that didn't need unravelling. He was always worrying about things that would never happen. He worried about buying a house. Both their families came from council homes and had their houses maintained on a regular basis. Hock worried that he would have to pay for his own repairs and maintenance. He'd admitted that he'd worried when Silvia had gone to Butlins, for that fated week's holiday with her friends, she would meet someone else. So he did it first.

When Silvia had returned home from holiday to find her Grandmother had died suddenly and Hock confessed he'd been out with someone else while she was away, she was devastated. He said he had worried so much that Silvia might fancy his best friend Whit more than him so "he chucked her" and gave Whit her telephone number.

Silvia was heartbroken but as punishment to Hock, when Whit called her, Silvia humoured him and went out with Whit for a few weeks. He had an offer of another job in another town but was undecided what to do in view of the fact that he was now seeing Silvia. Silvia advised him to go. Her heart wasn't in the relationship, she had exams to study for and the person she most admired had found himself someone else.

Twelve months later Silvia had left school and landed the job in The Totally Boring Insurance Company. It was the last Thursday of the month - pay day. Silvia and Mona were going out to celebrate. They headed for their favourite club, famous for its flooding at high tide and everyone being locked in until the small hours until the tide went out. You could see the Liverpool skyline lit up across the river and the Liver Buildings reflected on the Mersey when there was a full moon.

They had a great night dancing till their stiletto's crushed their feet and they could stand no more. They made a pact that they would leave ten minutes before the end to avoid the now sweaty men leering towards unsuspecting females for the last dance and hopefully tap off before home time, and to avoid the queue at the cloakroom.

 As they made their way towards the exit a familiar, his smiling face stepped into her view. It was Hock. He had been there all night watching her from a distance and again she hadn't seen him. The chemistry between them was still powerful and overwhelming even after three months and they fell into each other's arms. He promised to call the next day and Silvia thought about him all day long. She couldn't wait to get home.

Silvia didn't have to wait long for her phone call from him either. On the stroke of 6pm the house phone rang and when she answered she heard the familiar pips at the other end of someone inserting their pennies into the slot of the public phone box until the correct amount had been reached and then they were allowed to speak and speak they did, for hours.

The Totally Boring Insurance Company had a direct line into their London branch. When the light flashed on the switchboard she had to answer it immediately. It was like the hot line to God. The voice at the other end asked to speak to Mr. Brayon.

"We don't have a Mr. Brayon," Silvia told the voice.

"No, not Mr. Brayon, Mr. Brayon," replied the voice.

"I'm sorry," said Silvia, "but we don't have a Mr. Brayon either.

"No, not Brayon, Brayon as in the colour Brayon!" exclaimed the voice, getting frustrated. Well, Silvia had never heard a cockney accent before either.

It was Silvia's job to make the coffee in the morning, tea in the afternoon, as is protocol in England and wash the dishes afterwards. Trying to remember who had milk and sugar out of 20 people was a memory task in itself. She made a list. She'd replaced a junior who went off to join the RAF as a radar technician - a skill she could have put to use in the office to scan for which one had the brain or a sense of humour.

Silvia felt constantly belittled by an "up-market type" called Petulant Pamela, who was only a clerk herself, but had a Father who owned his own insurance company and she was learning the ropes from Daddy's friend who'd taken her on board. Silvia soon realised that it wasn't what you knew but whom you knew that got you the job.

"I must have got the job because my Father was a Manager, and it sounds good," Silvia thought to herself, after remembering her interview.

"What does your Father do? What does your Mother do?" they asked.

"Why the hell do they want to know that?" Silvia thought. "They aren't going to work here." But it was all to separate the wheat from the chaff. "Father's a Manager, and Mother is a Supervisor," she informed them, and those two little words made all the difference. She didn't mention that one was with a flooring company, that her Father would many years later come to own, and the other a chocolate factory belt supervisor. The fact they she lived on a council estate (a very nice one mind, where everyone looked after their properties) didn't seem to matter.

Petulant Pamela would thrust an envelope in Silvia's direction and without even looking her in the eye would demand that she take it round to General Slips, Trips & Accidents Insurance Co. around the corner. She was higher up the echelons than Silvia, so answering back was not the respectful thing. "Stuff that for a game of soldiers," Silvia thought, "she'll get a piece of my mind whether she likes it or not one of these days!" So Silvia would put on her coat in all weathers and walk around the block to the General Slips, Trip and Accidents Insurance Co. to deliver the letter.

Silvia didn't have to wait long for revenge. Petulant Pamela's paunchy husband, Grubby Graham, had a suspected affair only a few weeks after their lavish marriage ceremony. He claimed his car had broken down and he had to stay the night at a friend's house who was so poor he didn't have a phone - mobiles where not invented then - and there were no public phone boxes for miles.
"Now you see how it feels to be upset by someone," Silvia thought to herself.

What goes around comes around, and Silvia didn't even have to open her mouth, but once again fate drew the final straw when Silvia misheard something her boss had said to her when someone cracked a joke and she was too busy laughing.
"Excuse me, I didn't quite hear that," Silvia queried.
"I said be quiet!" demanded the wrinkly fossil with the grey skin and bad teeth from smoking too much.

Silvia was stunned. Her lower jaw dropped four inches as she gazed at him gormlessly in amazement.

"What kind of dickhead didn't like the sound of laughter?" Silvia mused. She was infuriated, "I don't believe this," she said disbelievingly, "I work my butt off for 10 weeks, answering a switchboard, filing claims and reminders, doing the post and working with snobs who don't laugh, enough is enough. And all this hassle for £11 a week!" – which was a lot of money in 1974.

"Stuff this, time to move on," she thought to herself with her mouth gaping open like a blown safe. She went after another job the next day, left on the Friday and started work on the Monday and instantly increased her salary by 50%. Karma.

PEOPLE ALWAYS NEED SECRETARIES

Silvia's new job was much more laid back. It was with a theatrical agency, run by two oddballs Mr. Paranoid and Mr. Neurotic. She started work at 10am and finished at 6pm, took calls from budding artistes and booked acts into local nightspots. She made friends quickly with the other girl they had employed, PR Pauline but they weren't allowed to lunch together as one of them had to cover the phones.

On one occasion a famous Liverpool comedian came into the office to sign contracts – all wild hair and buck teeth. Pauline whisked him away to their "posh" offices upstairs for the champagne celebration.

Once a week it was audition night at a local social club. They would attend and listen to budding artistes hoping to make a living singing or playing an instrument, or both. Silvia took a call from a well-spoken, elderly lady asking if they need a penis!

"I'm sorry," Silvia asked, embarrassed, "do we need a what?"
"A penis."
"I'm sorry this is a theatrical agency, we book acts into clubs. I think you need the escort agency downstairs,"
"No, no dear, I play the piano. I'm a pianist."
"Oh," said Silvia blushing and thinking she must get her hearing checked!

"There's a hearing consultant in the shop at the front of the building, I'll make an appointment with them," she informed herself.

She'd got to know Mary, the consultant's assistant, quite well over recent weeks. All the offices shared a kitchen and Mary would often pop her head around the door to see how Silvia was doing. A nice, smiley face with a sense of humour - at last she could laugh freely.

Silvia's room was at the side of the building and had no window, so she was relieved to see daylight from time to time when she ventured down the hallway to the shop at the front. It had a huge plate glass window that let all the sunshine in from the other side of Bold Street and Mary was always on her own after 11am when the pub round the corner opened. Her boss, a nervy type, used alcohol in moderate quantities to calm his tremors.

"He's never been the same since his wife gave birth," Mary told Silvia. "I think he suffered psychosomatic pregnancy and developed an ulcer. He thinks the beer relieves the pain."

So most lunchtimes Silvia spent her time with Mary, eating her lunch on the sofa in the shop, where the sun shone through the window.

By now Mr. Paranoid and Mr. Neurotic were beginning to get paranoid and neurotic over the escort agency in the basement, "Big Boobs and Bums Escort Agency". With frequent visitors for escorts at all hours of the night and massage and saunas during the day, they were worried about the effect it would have on their business. Silvia couldn't see what the problem was. Most of their bookings were done on the phone and the auditions were held miles away, but when she came in one day to find Mr. Neurotic popping pills after he'd found a steaming turd on the lavatory floor and ranting like a lunatic, "It was one of their customers that had left it," he pointed towards the stairs, shaking his hands with such rage it made his thick and heavy silver wrist bangles rattle like a snake's tale in the desert, that Silvia decided it was perhaps time again to move on.

"OK fate, I can take a hint," she said looking upwards.

She confided in Mary about her intensions and Mary told her that her boss needed someone, although he wasn't aware of it yet.

"He's got behind with his invoicing and no money is coming in. He needs someone to sort him out," she said and arranged a meeting with him and Silvia.

So Silvia moved up in the world - or at least to the front of the building where she could sit on the sofa in the warm sunshine. She was now working as a secretary for a prestigious company, "Mutt'n'Jeff Hearing Consultants", whose owner Mr. Normal lived in a turreted house overlooking the Wirral Bay peninsula - and earned herself a whopping pay rise to £18 a week, a lot of money back then.

So it isn't what you know but whom you know networking theory that was now working for Silvia.

Silvia typed his invoices, answered his phone, served his customers, made his appointments and discovered his empty brandy bottles and scantily clad lady magazines in his desk drawers all over the office.

Every morning she would hear the screw top of the bottle unwinding as he took his first glug to keep him going until the pub opened at 11am. He'd return again at 3pm slightly sozzled but in a jovial mood and wolf down the sandwiches, which Mary would bring in for him everyday - and for which he never paid her. The poor, feeding the rich.

Silvia reflected on the sad mornings with him and happy afternoons with Mary. It would break her heart to leave but she had to move on. Silvia and Hock had been seeing each other for two years and had become engaged with intentions to marry and she needed more money if they were to set up home together. She was earning £16 a week – a lot of money in 1976, but not enough.

It was a happy relationship and they were inseparable but was it right to be thinking of settling down at the grand old age of eighteen to a man who was troubled about paying a mortgage and repairs on a house.

"Why should we pay when the council would do it for us if we lived in one of their houses just like our parents do?" he discussed with her.

"But we'd end up paying rent for the rest of our lives if we did but if we had our own house we wouldn't and could be rent free," she replied.

But he also had other issues as well. For some reason he was troubled about the Russians invading - well it was 1976 and with the presence of the "Russian Woodpecker" Duga-3, America was in a standoff with Russia, so maybe he had a point.

MOVING ON UP

Silvia arrived at a tall office building in the financial district behind James Street Station and took the lift to the 8th floor, Engineering Department of "Far East Freight Shifters Ltd". It was her first day and she was introduced to her new colleagues, Eve, Christlyne and Joan.

It was an inner office with no sunshine and bitterly cold in the winter months, the only heating being buried in the walls of the building and covered by huge drapes that she had to pile up on the window ledges to let some warmth radiate from the plaster and reach her back.

She worked for a department of engineers who had all been to sea themselves but were now considered unseaworthy in one form or another either through illness or being too old to stay away from their families for long periods of time. One guy had diseased hands due to an allergy to the oil he worked with and was shipped back to Liverpool and desk job duties.

Silvia had applied for the job through the recommendation of a friend of her Grandmother Olive, who cleaned for a lady with severe arthritis and was mainly bedridden. Olive had mentioned Silvia to her and discovered that she used to work for a shipping company and still knew people there and could 'have a word' with someone to find out if they needed any staff. Silvia spent an hour and a half in the interview, the longest yet, explaining her position and herself and how she wanted and needed to move on. She got the job. "After all, it isn't what you know but whom you know," she smiled to herself at her achievement.

She settled into the mundane routine of typing lists of nuts, bolts and screws while trying to save for a wedding on the massive salary increase to £20 a week, a lot of money in 1976. At least it will help pay the mortgage.

The office was never warm enough and neither were the girls, even with a twin-set on and a large wrap cardigan over the top of them. Joan, the eldest of them all, used to insist on having the window open to clear her stuffy nose and even on cold, blustery days would take a hike down to the Pier Head for a brisk walk in her Rosa Klebb shoes on the insistence that it was her doctor's recommendation that it would help strengthen the weak veins in her nose and stop the nose-bleeding. Christlyne's hands used to turn so blue with the cold, due to poor circulation, that they regularly used to joke about checking her wrist for a pulse.

"If she doesn't shut that bleedin' window, I'll make her nose bleed," shivered Christlyne.

On the frequent days that Joan called in sick due to a terrible cold that had mysteriously descended upon her during the early hours, and she couldn't figure out why, and it couldn't possibly be anything to do with the freezing temperature in the office due to her open window policy, Silvia called down to the typing pool to request a replacement.

A tall, jolly girl called Hilby arrived and took her place in Joan's seat. She had a pleasing personality and fitted in straight away. Hilby was a few years older,
with no boyfriend as yet, and gossiped with the girls about why there were so many older, single ladies in the office.

The company had some out-dated rules and regulations and was a little over the top when it came to married women working. It had only recently accepted that women no longer had to give up their jobs when they married; they could manage both. They no longer had to cover their arms in the office; sleeveless dresses had become fashionable in the 60's, and the no trousers rule was a little out-dated. It was 1976 NOT 1966! The company was full of unmarried maidens and spinsters - many of an age nearing retirement, who had forgone the chance of marriage in favour of a job. Joan was one of them.

"Well," Silvia informed everyone, "I don't know about you, but that ain't gonna happen to me! There's no way I'm staying home to look after the house while the husband's out all day at work. I want my own money and don't want to have to rely on him for a few miserly pennies to spend on making myself look nice for when he comes home from work." Silvia was not going to be one of those women.

Eve was the first to announce that she was getting married - to an engineer she'd met at work. A hen party was organised with a coach trip to a fancy nightclub in Manchester – Pips, behind the Cathedral, the ad on the telly used to say. They were all Cinderella's having a ball when Eve went missing. They searched the two floors and the ladies loos looking for her. They'd never have believed in a million years that anything bad could happen - stuff like that just doesn't happen to young girls out innocently enjoying themselves.

The boys here looked different, smarter. Silvia's head was turned by a handsome, suited character (Hock always wore jeans) who danced with her to Stevie Wonder's 'Isn't she lovely'. Why was that when she was supposed to be in love with Hock and him with her? They had been arguing a lot more recently and he'd gone off with his friends to Stonehenge for a dipping with the Druids and to witness the rising of the Sun on the summer solstice - he was getting into some odd things lately. And of course he couldn't phone her because the only phones were in the garage where he filled up with petrol.

Silvia realised she was getting fed up at playing house with him when their parents were away, she was fed up with doing the shopping on her way home, carrying heavy shopping bags on the train and cooking his meals for him when she got home.
"He was home first, why couldn't he cook a meal for me?" Silvia thought. "That was a fairer deal."

The beginning of the cracks came when they were going to a New Year's Eve party and Silvia was all dressed up and ready when he knocked on the door. Silvia's Father answered and let Hock in. He took one look at Silvia and said, "You're not wearing that are you?" Silvia went back upstairs and changed to keep the peace but her Father told her later that he thought she looked lovely and she should never have gone back and changed what she was wearing.
Silvia knew he was right, her respect for Hock was waning and so it seemed was her Father's, and he was becoming argumentative and picky since he'd learned to drive.

Silvia travelled on the train to work everyday and paid her own fares. Hock used the car to go to work. During the summer he told Silvia he wasn't very well and started taking days off sick. Silvia discovered that he was ferrying his friends to the beach every day for a swim and building up a great sun tan, not something you get lying in bed sick. When he asked her for money for petrol her words were harsh but straight to the point.
"I am not paying you to ferry your friends around, you fucker. I can't even drive the car let alone use it! I pay my own fares to work. You earn twice the amount I do. If you want money ask your friends for it and see how long they stick around then!" Silvia screamed at him at a frighteningly audible level that almost made his ears bleed and set the neighbourhood dogs barking.

Hock was in shock, which would have been an abbreviation of Silvia's name if she married him. S.Hock. She'd never answered him back before and thanked God her name wasn't Phyllis. (P.Hock).

She was fed up of being taken advantage of. They never went on holiday as they were supposed to be saving up to get married and all he'd suggested was a weekend camping trip in North Wales, carrying all the gear on the train themselves, before they got the car.

As good a trip as it was, package holidays were beginning to take off and a holiday in the sun was just what Silvia wanted and camping wasn't her idea of a restful holiday or conducive to the happy married life to come, if this is was what it was gong to be like. It seemed these days the only one who was glad to see her was her Father, who ran up the hallway to greet her when he heard the key in the door and to give her a big hug. Why couldn't she meet someone like her dad? Smart, and with polished shoes.

So Mr. Suited and Booted was a sight for sore eyes and a pleasant change from being used, he enjoyed dancing, which Silvia loved too. Hock didn't dance. He preferred to stand at the bar with a pint and look 'cool' chatting and smoking with his friends. Silvia began to have doubts. Her thoughts were rudely interrupted and there wasn't an opportunity to swap phone numbers with him.

Eve had reappeared safely, and announced to the hen party's probing questions, "I just wanted a last fling before I got married and went down the entry at the side of Pips with some bloke who showed an interest in me. Robert's always away at sea and never seems bothered these days what I do."

Silvia thought she meant a kiss and realised how naive she'd been when Eve dragged her into the ladies and asked for help to get a mysterious white gooey stain out of her chiffon frock.

"What's that?" Silvia asked her.

"He dribbled." Eve told her.

Silvia was stunned. How could she do such a thing? She was supposed to be marrying the man she loved, it didn't make sense to Silvia, she was old fashioned in that way and believed in one-man one woman and no funny stuff.

"I can't let Robert see this," she said, I need to clean it off before I get home." But Silvia knew that it wouldn't completely come out unless it was given a good scrub with soapy water. All cleaned up as best they could with a paper towel and some hand soap, dried off under the hand dryers, they boarded the coach back to the Wirral stopping off at Burtonwood services on the M62 at 3am for a beans on toast breakfast followed by an almond tart and a cup of tea. It was daylight when she was dropped off safely back home, thinking of the suit.

The following week Eve married Robert and they were all invited to the evening do in the posh place of the decade, the Devon Doorway. Silvia spent hours doing her hair and put on her prettiest dress and waited for Hock to pick her up. When he arrived he looked smart, no jeans just nicely pressed trousers and a shirt, but then Silvia noticed that there was some fraying on his sleeves and when she looked closer she could see that the seams had given way and were exposing the flesh on his arms. Silvia couldn't believe it. He'd always been clean and tidy but this was unacceptable. It was like he didn't want to go to the wedding and couldn't be bothered making the effort for her anymore. This would be the first time her work friends would meet him and they'd see his clothes in this state. "You can't go out like that," Silvia told him incredulously, and got out her sewing kit and proceeded to mend the offending fissures as best she could. She asked him to role up his sleeves so they could get a move on.

A few nights later, when Silvia was sitting home alone, her Father came in from his golf club in Hoylake and shouted her name not expecting a reply.

"I'm in here!" she shouted back from the sitting room.

"Oh, I thought you were out with Hock?"

"Not tonight dad, he's out with his friend," she answered, disappointed. It seemed that they were drifting apart and nothing she did made any difference. It seemed the more she tried the more he backed away. He'd even started complaining about what she ate and drank and that he hated the smell of coffee on her breath. No mention though of his ashtray breath, because he smoked. Silvia refused to stop drinking it, why should she? It was him who'd changed not her!

Belinda rang her a few weeks later. She was now working for a large catalogue company in Liverpool and she'd overheard a conversation in the ladies toilets at work and was concerned. A girl she vaguely knew was talking about this lovely bloke she'd met in the local pub and he'd taken her out for a drink in Hoylake. His name was Hock and he had his own car. It was around the time he said he'd been at Stonehenge but it was too much of a coincidence.

There was no escaping the fact now that Hock had a roving eye and Silvia wasn't going to play second fiddle to anyone. She'd rather suffer a broken heart for a few months than a lifetime of arguing and humiliation.

So when she accidently dropped a box of eggs into his trainers in the pantry one night, while attempting to cook his dinner, it sparked off one unholy row. During his frantic raving and spluttering to get his words out, Silvia just looked at him and burst out laughing, mimicking him. She had finally realised what a pathetic tosspot he was. He was seriously chucked. She never cleaned up the eggs, packed her bag and caught the bus home. He didn't try to stop her. She didn't want him to. He hadn't even had the decency to chuck her when he'd met someone new. How she wished she'd got Mr. Suited and Booted's phone number now.

When Silvia told her Mother she was now young, free and single, Silvia's Mother informed her that her Father thought he had seen Hock that night he was on his way back home from the golf club, in their car with another girl but he thought it was Silvia, so was surprised to find her still at home.

Why hadn't they had told her sooner, who were they trying to protect - their own daughter or Hock, she could have ended her agony sooner. She knew what she wanted from a man but her Mother thought she was too fussy. She wasn't fussy she just had standards - and no one to fill them. The Cold War was over. She wasn't cut out to be a Stepford Wife or a doormat.

Silvia found the hardest thing was closing down the joint account they'd set up to save for the wedding, she needed his signature. Hock went round to Silvia's Mother's to sign the document while she was away on holiday explaining sheepishly that they would be alright. They were still friends. "Friends my arse," Silvia said and never saw him again.

BOREDOM SETS IN

Still without a boyfriend for company, Silvia took a bar job in her local pub down the road, working for Mr. Nasty Bastard at the "Beer Swiller's Watering Hole". She worked 4 nights a week for £10 after tax to supplement her salary and help pay for future package holidays to Ibiza and Majorca, which were becoming popular. She hadn't had a holiday abroad before that involved two weeks of sunbathing and still couldn't swim after a disastrous attempt at New Brighton baths put her off for life when her cousin promised to catch her at the bottom of the slide and didn't. Silvia went right under and every orifice filled with water. She couldn't see, she couldn't breathe, she couldn't hear. She managed to scramble out coughing and spluttering and ran to her Mother crying. She never went near the water again, until now.

Belinda and Silvia went down to the local swimming baths, where to her surprise an old school friend was the lifeguard. He told her what she needed to do to gain confidence in the water.
"Just hold your nose and dip your head under, you're not going to drown as your feet are on the floor," he instructed.
Silvia did as she was told, and he was right, she didn't drown.
"Now you're in the shallow end so all you have to do is put your feet down to stop, so push off with your feet and move your arms and legs," he carried on.
To Silvia's amazement she began to swim, underwater, but she could swim!

One night she was serving in the lounge - Silvia hated the lounge, it was too quiet, she much preferred the bar with the lively banter or the music room with the jukebox and bands. An old lady, who sat in the same corner every night with a gin and tonic because she was too scared to stay in her own home after being burgled, took a turn for the worse and keeled over off her chair. An ambulance was called and when the flashing blue lights could be seen through the windows the shout went up that Mr. Nasty Bastard had died and the whole pub cheered. He'd earned his name by shouting, "Ok we've had your money, now fuck off home!" at closing time.
It was hard graft and after two years of using it for the holiday fund and a social life Silvia finally called it a day when he accused her of taking money from the till. From where he was standing he could only see a few numbers on the till display and made Silvia hold her hand out so

he could check the change. She was right, he was wrong, he never apologised, she left.

Silvia knew that she needed more training if she wanted to get herself another job. She took shorthand lessons but hated it so much that she began to play truant from night school classes. So to cheer herself up she went on a shopping spree to spending her well-earned extra £10 a week.

POISON DWARFO

Silvia had just finished writing to a top fashion retailer 'Tall and Lanky Gits Attire' to complain about the range of clothes available to women under five foot three inches in their Poison Dwarfo section. She was astonished to find that in the 'Tall and Lanky Gits Attire' range there was a vast variety of flowing gowns in a deluge of summery colours.

Silvia had stood in front of the dressing room mirror, five foot two and three quarters in her flip-flops. There were three mirrors in the cubicle, designed to give a front and back view from all angles. She started in disbelief. Who was in the cubicle with her? She spun around to find no one there. The wobbly bum belonged to her. Nothing fitted. Skirts and trousers were too long and rested in folded piles around her ankles. "I'd need to cut six inches off all these," she thought, "and that would ruin the shape."
"Any good, Madam?" purred the assistant.

Silvia remembered the time when she was a kid and smock dresses were all the rage for teenagers. Mona managed to beat her to the last one in the shop and the hunt was on then for the next best thing. After trawling round town for hours they came across a decent one in a boutique of some reputation stocking "women's sizes". After trying it on, it hung on her like a Mama Cass (Google it) after a crash diet. The assistant stepped into the changing room to admire her next sale.
"Oh, it looks lovely," she gushed, holding it in at the back. "It really suits you."
The shoulders were down to her elbows and the neck slid up towards her chin as the back slid down her back with the weight of the fabric. But it was the only one and she was desperate. She bought it, it was expensive and Silvia regretted it for the rest of her teenage years as she never did grow into it and wasn't going to fall into that trap again.

"Too long," answered Silvia handing them back with a humph.
"Oh, you need our Dwarfo collection, these are our Tall and Lanky stock," the assistant smirked.

Silvia proceeded to the Petite section - aptly named for dwarfos like Silvia - but not one suitable garment in the same style could be found. In fact, the only items available were all dull browns (not Silvia's colour) or leopard and tiger prints - OK if you're an aging rock star or married to one - but not exactly what Silvia would deem respectable for the office, and not a pretty colour in sight.

She asked the manager at the 'Hand over your dosh here' counter when the new range for short arses would be arriving only to be told that it wouldn't until the existing drab stock was shifted. Incensed at the prospect of buying a decent frock for fifty quid and having to cut six inches off the bottom, Silvia compiled a petition and sent one to all her dwarfo friends, with the fax number of the marketing department of the company concerned in large type at the top, requesting they fill it in along with all their friends, relatives and colleagues of the same disposition and send it off, pronto! Social media had not yet been invented.

Silvia figured it wouldn't be long before 'Tall and Lanky Gits Attire' were inundated with recycled trees and forced to sack their buyers for stocking their 'Short and Almost Forced To Go Naked Because I've Got Nothing To Wear' departments with the drabbest clothes since the Russian revolution.

Silvia was forced to buy the long frock down to her ankles and mused as to what she should do with the left over six inches of white linen cut from the hemline. She could make a headband that Alice in Wonderland would be jealous of, or she could mail it to 'Tall and Lanky Gits Attire' demanding a refund for the wastage. Silvia had never had this much trouble deciding what to do with an extra six inches before! She decided the best place for it was in the bin. She'd also never considered herself hard to shop for but found it increasingly difficult as she got older - she was fast approaching thirty.

When Silvia was in primary school she was considered one of the tallest in her class and was always placed on the back row of school photographs with the other tall kids. But as she progressed through school she noticed she was slowly descending the ranks of uniformity to eventually end up on the front row, cross-legged with all the other dwarfos. By this time there were so many of them that the school photographer had trouble placing them all.

Silvia blamed her dilemma on the school milk and assumed that the Government must be experimenting with growth hormones again and forgotten to put her quota in her allocated free, half pint recommended daily allowance.

At the tender age of twelve, the fashion world had been turned up side down when the mini skirts of the sixties turned into the midi skirts of the seventies. Suddenly everyone was tripping over their coats and slipping on the heels of their white plastic boots. The club heels gave Silvia the added height she needed but the elastication round the tops turned her knees blue when they cut off her circulation. To complete the ensemble Silvia wore a long, black Midi coat with the biggest brass buttons you'd ever seen, so much so that the local church took bookings for coach trips to come and do brass rubbings.

She was glad when the free milk stopped. She feared that if she drank any more she would end up shrinking down to a speck of dust on the carpet!

Twelve months after the purchase at 'Tall and Lanky Gits Attire', Silvia still hadn't worn the damn dress!

NEW BEGINNINGS

Changes came at work, too. There was talk of redundancies but she'd
been offered two promotions but wasn't sure how long the jobs would
last and had turned them down, they were both in the accounts
department and although good at Maths she didn't want to number
crunch all day, every day.
"How about in the telex room?" her boss asked.
"Too noisy. It sound like the Pools computer on a Saturday night
clicking out the results, only 10 times louder and all day long," she
informed him.

"What about VDU?" (Visual display units as computers were called
back then and not some horrible infection) he suggested.
"I'll go bog eyed looking at that thing all day!"

Finally, it was actually doing the job she was already doing but she
renegotiated the pay grade to get it upgraded - with a pay rise for all of
the girls included into the bargain - when she happened to read the job
description and discovered they were doing half the things on the next
pay grade anyway. So they were all instantly rewarded with a massive
pay rise to £30 a week a lot of money in 1978, but now she had no
mortgage to save up for.

Hilby, Christlyne and Silvia became great friends, even holidaying
together on a wine tasting tour around Germany and France, and
progressing to a 10-day trip to the South of France by coach, ferry and
train, later that year.

Even though Hilby always returned to the typing pool Silvia always requested that it be her who covered for staff off sick, but when Eve finally left to be a lady of leisure after her marriage to her engineer, Hilby joined the department permanently. They were complete - three musketeers against the Fossil who still wouldn't close the window of their office as the trees shivered their leaves to the ground with the onset of autumn and the approaching depths of winter again.

The South of France sounded so glamorous, and expensive, but not if you went in September when all the kids had gone back to school. The weather was still nice and warm enough to walk around in shorts and a T-shirt during the day and balmy in the evenings.

Their destination was going to be St. Aygulf on the French Riviera, in a small complex, which consisted of a circular building hosting the reception, dining room, family entertainment room and a disco in the basement. The grounds housed rows of old army barrack looking buildings of bedrooms with shower rooms at the end of each row – one end for the ladies and the other end for the gents.

They would need some glamorous clothes to match and some decent shoes for all the sightseeing in Cannes and Nice and with the upgrade in their salaries they could now afford both.

On a cool September morning in England they set off on the train from Liverpool to London, crossed London to Victoria Coach Station and panicked when they couldn't find the coach and thought they must have missed it.

There was no gate number on their tickets to tell them where they should be waiting and no signposts to inform them where they need to be. Fortunately Hilby spotted someone dragging a suitcase and politely asked them if they knew where their trip was leaving from. They pointed her in the direction of their rep, an elderly gentleman helping to load the cases onto the coach.

"Phew," Silvia sighed in relief, "we thought you'd gone without us."
He was to be their tour guide throughout the trip.

The coach departed and headed for Dover, where they all embarked
for the crossing and disembarked in Bologne for the train station and
the overnight sleeper to Nice. They searched for their couchette birth
and found they were sharing it with a woman and her two young boys.

While Hilby and Christlyne settled in for the night, Silvia went to
investigate the buffet car for a drink and a snack for them all. She
opened the door and heard music and laughter; there was a disco and
people dancing. She pushed her way through to the bar and bought
some crisps and cans and practically ran back to the couchette to get
them up and out again. They danced and got talking to others staying
at the same place as them. They were exhilarated with expectation of
the beautiful places they were about to see.

The next morning the cabin crew knocked on their door at 7am and
one by one they trolled off to the bathroom to freshen up for the day.
They would soon be arriving in Nice where the coach would take them
to St. Aygulf after a brief stop in St. Raphael.

Their first night consisted of a sumptuous meal with wine, the upstairs
for the family entertainment and more sparkling wine – cheap at 16
francs a bottle, and finally at 11am when the kids went to bed all the
adults would head down to the basement for the disco. And so it
continued every night for the next 7 nights.

Days were spent sightseeing in Grasse, the home of the great
perfumeries, Nice and Cannes or spending free days on the local
beaches where they met a young Robert Redford look-a-like, who took
a shine to Silvia. He could speak no English and her only a few words
of French she learned in school, so they used another from their party
as an interpreter. He wanted to take her out for the evening, so they

met after the evening meal and he took her in his car for a drive around the coast road.

They spent the evening in silence or mumbled Franglish to try and understand each other while watching a parachutist come down in the bay while the sunset. He drove her to the beach the next day and took a photo of her sitting posing on a rock, with her slender legs on display. That night they made love on the beach, and she told him she was not going to see him again because she was on holiday with her friends.

Silvia returned to the complex just in time for the disco to start, and the wine to be opened. By closing time they were hungry again and were told to go to the bar in the village, which served baguettes until the early hours. The service was painfully slow and it was 3am by the time they all got back to their room, which consisted of a single bed and bunk beds and Silvia was on the top.

That morning they awoke with the light still on and covered in crumbs from the baguettes they had tried to eat in bed before dozing off.

***

By the time spring arrived, Silvia knew she wouldn't take another winter in that office.
"I need to look for another job and there's talk of redundancies again," she told her friends.
"Why do you think it would be you they made redundant?" they asked.
"I can't take the risk by staying and I'm losing interest fast. I need to move on, but we'll stay in touch you can guarantee it," she explained and she meant it.

That Thursday night she bought the Liverpool Echo on the way home and browsed through the classifieds. There were four potential jobs she could apply for. She applied for them all and got interviews with two. One was at a prestigious garage in West Kirby, who had addressed the envelope to Silvia but the letter inside was to someone else - did she want to work for a company that makes mistakes like that? Nope. The other was with an advertising agency in Liverpool. "Go On - Buy It, Advertising & Marketing".

Silvia had read an article in Cosmo a few months before, about a woman working in an advertising agency. It was pitching for a new account (roll-on deodorant). She came up with a catch phrase. They won the account; she was promoted to copywriter and given a Porsche, easy as that.

When she applied for the job she was interviewed by the PA and had a second interview with John Lennon look-a-like. He had a huge office with a TV - to watch the commercials they made. His drinks cabinet was always fully stocked and the cigar bill for the month was over £1000. She took a typing test in 20 minutes on a big, green Hermes chunky keyed typewriter, just like the one she learnt on in school, made no mistakes and got the job, easy as that. Silvia was informed that out of 70 applicants, she was the only one that hadn't made a mistake on her typing test. She was so proud.

She set off to work the following Monday in a snow blizzard. By the time she arrived at the office she was covered in melting snowflakes glistening in her curly brown hair. It was 10th April and she was now earning £33 a week - a lot of money in 1979.

WORK, REST AND PLAY

On her first day she was shown around the office and introduced to people having 'standing on their head' competitions, to see who could last the longest without passing out or turning blue, people singing at the top of their voices to the radio and riding around the office on their bikes.

"Now this is more like it," Silvia whispered to herself.

She called everybody by their first names and not their last ones. She had an instant social life - Thursday night was pay day and a pub crawl was not optional it was compulsory, they took her on a tour of back alleys, through narrow doorways, down steps into cellars which opened into huge rooms full of bustling bodies and rock bands playing and by the end of the first week Silvia had a new boyfriend, too. Scouse Lad.

Weekdays were great, the people were great, and her social life was great. But at the weekends Silvia was lonely. Scouse Lad always seemed to be doing something most weekends and she saw him infrequently when she had the most time. Weekends were boring places to be - give Silvia the working week any day. Roll on that Monday morning feeling with the hilarious pranks, of glueing a fake European Football match ticket to the pavement outside and watched drunken foreign fans trying to pick it up.

Promotion after promotion every two years was hard earned. Silvia applied for job after job as soon as she heard someone was leaving she would put in her application.

"It isn't as though I'm leaving to go somewhere else, just another floor or office but still be working with the same people, so it's ideal," she told her boss, the John Lennon look-alike. He agreed and she'd get the job. Silvia felt she was now working for a company that recognised her worth.

When he left to set up his own business in London, he brought in a new guy, Mr. Super Tosspot and every time Silvia applied for a new role he turned her down because she didn't have a university degree, and they employed someone else. Silvia was gutted, that had never happened before, people believed in her and she knew she could do the job. So she bided her time and carried on as normal.

When it was pay rise time, Mr. Super Tosspot called her in to discuss her remuneration package for the following year.

"I'll give you an extra £500," he offered. Silvia pulled a face and before she could say anything he spluttered, "OK £1000 then!"

Silvia hadn't even opened her mouth but was quick to fathom that just a look at the right time, with a weak-willed boss could get you what you wanted! Silvia had found his weak spot and she smiled to herself. Who needed a bloody degree with her negotiating skills? Karma. Now earning £53 a week, which was a lot of money in 1981.

"Ha ha, what a thicko!" Silvia laughed, as she left his office a whole lot richer, but not really realising what just happened, "that's the most money I've earned without actually saying anything, and he's the one with the university degree, but for someone of his standing he knows nothing about the behavioural aspects of marketing or how to keep a poker face when doing deals himself." She'd doubled her salary rise in 10 minutes! The next time a promotion came up Silvia got it.

When Scouse Lad decided to leave the company she knew it would be the last time she would see him. She felt sad but not as sad as she thought she might be, and once he was safely out of the way a new love interest stepped into the limelight appearing to her in a way she'd never thought of him before.

They'd been friends of a sort and travelled part of the way home from work together on the train; he lived in North Wales and changed trains at Bidston. They talked a lot about a lot of things and they laughed together. He knew her already and Silvia liked him. His name was Passionate Pete.

On the night Scouse Lad had his leaving do in the pub next door, Passionate Pete was there waiting in the background. Silvia got tipsy but he made sure she got on the train home safely, but not before she felt a slight tug on her arm as he escorted her up the side street of the pub.

"Where are we going?" asked Silvia giggling. "The station's that way!" She pointed across the road. He didn't reply but just shoved her into a doorway and moved in for a kiss. Silvia wasn't sure what to make of it, but it was so passionately good and she was so surprised, that she grabbed his jacket and pulled him back in close to her, whispering his name and kissed him back, hard. As he moved away she held onto him for another and another, whispering his name in disbelief.

Silvia couldn't remember if they spoke at all on the journey home. She was stunned, what would she say to him on Monday. She had all Saturday and Sunday to wait - he'd never even asked her for her phone number so they could talk over the weekend. She was nervous.

A few days later she found herself sitting alone in the office, when she saw a figure approaching her desk. Silvia looked up and saw him standing there, nervous himself and knew what he was about to ask but just as he opened his mouth to get the words out her colleague came back to her own desk and the moment was lost - just at the point he was about to ask her to be his love, he was halted in his tracks and he moved silently away. Silvia was gutted. He never did pluck up the courage to ask her out and Silvia was to shy to ask him out.
"What if?" she sometimes wondered what would her life have been like if he had asked her.

Not one to outstay her welcome in a job and with the need to move on yet again Silvia decided to see what options were now open to her with her new experience in advertising and marketing, skills that could be transferrable to any industry.

Jobs were becoming scarce and all of a sudden they all had fancy titles that you couldn't understand anymore. Personnel Departments were now calling themselves Human Resources, Publicity Officers were now Public Relations, it was becoming harder to find new jobs to move on to and understand what it was she was applying for.

With her new found wealth, Silvia realised she could actually afford her own place, nothing grand as it was going to be just her and started looking for a small flat in New Brighton, near to the train station so she could still get to work easily.

She found a nice little attic flat on Warren Drive, with her own the entrance up a staircase around the back of the building. She took her Father to the viewing with her for advice. It was perfect, small open plan living room/kitchen dining and a separate bedroom and bathroom, ideal for a single person. Her Father was worried about the entrance being round the back, and dark in the winter and how they would get furniture up the 3-storey metal staircase which clung to the back of the building.

Silvia discussed it with her friend Justine, who was a nurse.
"I've been thinking of getting my own place," she said, "maybe we could buy a place together."
"Really," replied Silvia, "it would make sense and I could do with the company when you're not on shifts."
They went to look at a small 3-bed terrace in the same area up for sale for £12k. It had a sunny aspect and slopping floors, which was a worry and made them feel drunk. They made an appointment with their building societies to ascertain if they could get a mortgage.

"What if one of you gets married?" the Manager asked.
"We'd sell the house and the one that wasn't could buy one on her own or buy the other out if they wanted to stay in it," Silvia answered politely.
He frowned and declined her application. It wasn't acceptable for a woman
to have a mortgage of her own in 1981, it had to be undersigned by a bloody man. However fate had a different plan.

PRECIOUS LITTLE DIAMOND

Silvia didn't feel like going out for the night. She'd had two years of being chatted up by every desperate man on the Wirral and none of them to her liking.

"What was the point?" she uttered under her breath as she backcombed her hair and applied the green hair gel to the sides of her head over her ears. In one upward sweeping movement it glued her hair to her scalp and was guaranteed to keep the style fixed in place for the night - and most of the next day.

"Every time I fancy someone, he doesn't fancy me and vice versa."

Silvia wore very little makeup. She hated that gunged-up feeling that foundation gave her so she preferred to go barefaced. Her only indulgence being a good mascara. She'd remove the stopper in the top and get a good coating on the brush so her lashes appeared extra long and separated. Then she'd apply another coat just to make sure you could see them under the disco lights, she couldn't be bothered with false ones as they were so heavy she couldn't keep her eyes open with them on. A good smudging of brown eyeshadow and white highlighter, a bit of blusher and lashings of magenta lipstick which she blotted on a tissue to avoid getting it on her teeth. Not recommended. Silvia thought to herself, "If I ever get marooned on a desert island I hope to God I have my mascara with me.

She dressed and admired herself in the mirror. She was small but slender and pleased with the outcome. She borrowed her mum's car keys and drove off to collect her friend Justine.

They headed for their favourite spot, the Nelson pub, on Grove Road. If you were going out to tap off it was best to go there first to see what was on offer in a decent lighting and also get a look at the competition, so you knew what you were up against. Everyone went to the Nelson first, it was always packed and the best night was Monday as the clubs were free to get in.

It was a great marketing tool. The weekend over, your money for the week almost gone, but that Monday morning feeling never happened because all you could think about was getting to the Chelsea Reach down on New Brighton promenade on a Monday night. The excitement that drummed up stopped anyone throwing a sickie on a Monday morning.

Once in the Chelsea you could dance the night away till one in the morning, then drive down prom to the Grand Hotel for the last hour till two. It was a different clientele in the Grand, a little bit rougher and older, and that was just the women.

An older guy asked Silvia to dance and she politely refused. If there was one thing she couldn't stand it was beer breath and men too wobbly to stand up properly. When he leered towards her she was promptly rescued by Prince Charming offering, "D'ya wanna dance?"

Not stopping to think, she gracefully accepted and headed to the dance floor for the last "slowy" of the night.
"Hey! What's he got that I haven't?" slurred the drunk to her friend.
"Charisma?" offered Justine, as she managed to assess the hunk that had just dragged Silvia away.

He was tall and wearing a t-shirt which exposed his muscular arms. Good. He could dance in time. Very good. He was extremely good looking. Things were looking up. He started to tell Silvia about himself.
"I'm in the Royal Navy, on nuclear subs up at Faslane," he said with pride.
"I campaign for Nuclear disarmament," said Silvia, pulling his leg.
He frowned but said nothing more till the record had finished and the lights came on.
"Where do you live?" he enquired.
"Moreton," Silvia replied.
"So do I!" he exclaimed in amazement. "Just above the shops opposite the church."
"By Michael's chippy," informed Silvia, which was less than half a mile away.

The bouncers began to usher people out of the club.

"Best go," said Silvia. "See you."

Silvia and Justine left the club, descended the steps outside and walked over to Silvia's car parked on the opposite side of the road next to the embankment.

"I don't understand it," said Justine. "Why didn't he ask you out? You could see he clearly fancied you."

"Story of my life," sighed Silvia.

Just as they were getting in the car Silvia looked back at the club to see a handsome figure rush out of the door and frantically look to his left and right, up and down the street. Silvia guessed that he might just be looking for her. She raised her hand and waved. He saw her and came running over.

"Could you give me a lift?" he asked.

"OK," smiled Silvia.

"I'll just get my jacket out of my friend's car."

"OK."

As he ran off Justine and Silvia looked at each other and smiled.

"Well that's never happened before," Silvia said, amazed.

"Well he's certainly got a different approach from anyone else!" said Justine.

"Do you really campaign for Nuclear disarmament?" he said dismayed, when he returned.

"No," she laughed, "it was all I could think of at the time."

"Thank God for that, or I wouldn't be able to go out with you," he said relieved. "Where do you fancy going on Saturday?"

Different approach alright and quick!

Silvia woke the next morning and looked in the mirror. Her hair hadn't moved from the night before and she had a smile on her face, or she thought it was a smile on her face but it was just last night's magenta lipstick ingrained into her lips. She scratched her itching head and belly as she looked at herself and suddenly remembered her chance meeting with Her Majesty's Royal Navy. Now she really smiled. "What luck," she thought, "boy, oh boy!" And she hadn't even been bothered about going out or even trying to meet someone.

"Well they say romance happens when you least expect it," she smiled again.

She got herself ready for work, a quick wash of the three "F's" - face, fanny and feet, re-applied the mascara, blusher and lippy and set off to catch the bus to the station. She was lucky she lived on a main road and could see the bus coming down the Meols Stretch that gave her time to lock the front door and cross to the bus stop. There was no shelter, so she had to time it just right on a rainy day.

Once boarded she noticed people staring at her, if it had been one or two people then she probably wouldn't have even noticed being still a bit groggy from the late night before. But when everyone started to stare she checked her reflection in the bus window.

"Have I got lippy on my teeth?" she thought. "No. Have I smudged my mascara and look like Alice Cooper? No."

She could now see why everyone was so interested in her. The hair gel she had used the previous night had dyed her blonde highlights green and they must have thought they were looking at a real live punk rocker.

"Shit," she said through clenched teeth, " I should have washed my hair. Too late now."

Silvia's bus arrived at Leasowe station and she waited patiently for the train to Liverpool. Leasowe was one of those old fashioned stations with a waiting room on each platform and proper seats and heating. The bus had to cross over the railway lines to get to the bus stop. If the barriers were down Silvia knew she'd miss it because the bus driver would never let anyone off in case they ran across the lines instead of legging it over the bridge two steps at a time to arrive exhausted on the platform on the other side.

Today she was lucky; the engineer was still in his gatehouse. She knew she had at least a few minutes to walk back to the platform because it took him that long to get to the gates himself. It was his job to turn the huge wheel pulley that opened and closed the gates to block off the traffic and let the trains pass.

Silvia glanced down the track, you could see for miles in the distance. The lines ran in a straight line as far as the eye could see, in one direction Bidston station towards Liverpool and the other Moreton station passing Cadbury's chocolate factory and onto Meols in the distance and finally West Kirby, the end of the line.

She remembered the nights she used to phone Mona to tell her what time train she would catch from Moreton station when she lived in Berrylands Road. She'd walk round the corner and cut through the Bramble Way cul-de-sac and up the steps that led to the top of the railway bridge, duck under the railings and run across the road to the ticket office and down the steps onto the platform. Two minutes later having passed the whole length of Cadbury's factory and waving frantically at Mona - who would stand in the back room window waiting for the train to pass the bottom of her garden - she would arrive at Leasowe, walk round the corner to Mona's mum's bungalow and listen to Billy Paul singing "Me and Mrs. Jones" on Radio Luxemburg and other great gems.

Both their Mothers worked at Cadbury's and used to bring home huge boxes of goodies from the "Choc Shop", which sold the misshapes to the staff. One night Mona ate a whole packet of Creme Eggs and turned up for school next day looking like the inside of one. Not content with that she'd also washed it down with a bottle of fizzy cream soda pop and she was still the skinniest girl in the school.

"One thing you could never erase from memory," thought Silvia, "was the smell of a new batch of chocolate being mixed, the aroma oozing from the factory like an invisible genie escaping from Aladdin's lamp."

Silvia's thoughts were interrupted by the arrival of the train as it slowed to a stop. Passing overland through Bidston, Birkenhead North, where her Father was born, Birkenhead Park, (Conway Park station wasn't built then), speeding past gardens, conservatories, and bathroom windows lit up with silhouettes of people getting ready for work, showering, shaving and downstairs eating their breakfasts at their kitchen tables. Onto Hamilton Square then under the River Mersey to James Street and Moorfields, where Silvia alighted. The train continued on its journey to Lime Street and Central before completing the loop back to James Street and over to the Wirral again.

It was a short walk round the corner to Tithebarn Street and Silvia would arrive at work in minutes but not before stopping at Sayers for a floury ham batch to soak up last night's remnants of moss still on her tongue.
"Ah breakfast," she sighed as she took a huge bite, nearly taking a chunk out of her bright pink manicured nails, that matched the lipstick stains now adorning the edge of the sandwich. Half her face was covered in flour. Silvia worked for an advertising agency, so her hair would look quite normal once she stepped inside the office, and maybe even her face.

The office janitor, a retired navy man himself, was always in early to unlock the building and turn the heating on. He kept it ship shape. He had an office by the reception area where he kept all the stationery stock and slept on a bench in there during his lunch break. The day Silvia started he turned up in a white coat holding a clip board and asked, "Miss Fernsby? Would you come with me for your medical, please?"

"Weird," thought Silvia, "they never mentioned a medical at the interview."

As Silvia started to rise from her chair the other girls in the office stopped her. It was lucky for her they were there.

"He's having you on!" they all said in unison.

Silvia discovered many of his foibles in the weeks to follow. Every morning he used to award one of the female staff a cream bun for the best-dressed boobs of the day. He informed Silvia that her big-chested friend Pamela had beaten her by a nipple. There was no sex discrimination in those days.

She also learned to keep on his good side. If you upset him in any way you would suddenly discover that the soft toilet paper had been replaced with sterile sheets of IZAL. Hard, shiny squares of paper with practically no absorbency what so ever. These were totally useless for women at certain times of the month, and totally useless to all any other time, especially when the huge mystery, bend blocking turd was discovered in the gents. He came rushing out of the cubicle with a bright red face, seething with anger, screaming, "Some dirty bastard has left a great steaming turd down the loo, I've tried flushing it, bleaching it and it turned white but still wouldn't flush, I'm now going to have to beat it back with the brush handle!"

There followed several cartoon impersonations of the event scattered around the notice boards and a month on IZAL.

HM Royal Navy called her that night and they began a whirlwind romance as best they could over a weekend with him working away all week. They went to look at an apartment, on his suggestion, with a view to moving in together and settling down but by Christmas the strain was beginning to show. They decided to call it a day.

One night alone in the house Silvia received a phone call but there was no one there. She knew it was him, probably having second thoughts. She didn't call him back. A week later he rang again to see if they could meet up. They went for a walk on the beach and discussed what had happened.

"It was all too quick," he told her. "I know what we need," he said, "a holiday. Let's go on holiday."

Silvia was apprehensive but thrilled, a whole two weeks, together. They booked a holiday to Tenerife. It was a disaster. He wasn't really interested in Silvia at all and rebuffed all her advances. She was just a companion not a girlfriend, so she ended it before he broke her heart again.

"You should never go back," she thought to herself.

LOVE AND MONEY

Agency life was not as glamorous as people thought. New staff arrived every year and thought it was a glamorous job, where you met lots of famous people on photo shoots and filmed commercials in exotic places. Things didn't turn out that glamorous for Silvia. She spent most of her time correcting the graduate's spelling mistakes and covering for account executives who couldn't be bothered returning to work after boozy lunches.

Her job in the Media Department in a small office next to her boss, Mr. Drunk & Disorderly, drove her mad. All she could hear day in and day out was him clipping his nails with a pair of small nail clippers.

"How bloody quick do those nails grow?" she muttered under her breath.

The cleaners had found him collapsed in the plant pot in his office one evening, after he returned to work drunk in the late afternoon after she'd already left for the day, and on another occasion he even tried to get out of Silvia's car whilst she drove him home through the Mersey

Tunnel at 30 mph. He was clutching his chest; Silvia thought he was having a heart attack.

"What the hell's wrong? Do you want me to take you to Birkenhead General?" she screamed at him, herself panicking.

"No take me home," he calmly replied once they reached the other side.

When Silvia arrived home she was in a state of shock, her Mother asked what was wrong and when Silvia relayed the story her Mother insisted that they call his house to check everything was OK. After several long minutes of hearing the phone ringing at the other end, a sleepy voice finally answered the call. It was Mrs. Drunk & Disorderly. Silvia explained what had happened to her and described his panic attack in the tunnel, she said everything was OK and he was fast asleep in bed now but she would keep an eye on him during the night. The next morning he came into work late as though nothing had happened. Git.

It was then Silvia discovered that he wasn't alone. She realised now how he'd managed to keep his job all this time, the whole management structure was on alcohol to get them through the day, week, month. From the top rung of the ladder right down to Mr. Junior Executive but it wouldn't be long before their clients became degree educated and couldn't be bullshitted anymore. They were a dying breed, maybe they knew it and that's why they drank.

Over the next two years Silvia was to hear of the drunken hierarchy being found in the flowerpots in reception, asleep and prostrate on boardroom tables and conked out in the gents loo with their pants round their ankles and faces pressed up against the door, arse still on the toilet seat so you couldn't get in to rescue them.

It even went as high as the Chairman and it was a revelation to discover that he had also lost his driving licence and had to be chauffeured around. All meetings of a serious nature had to take place before lunchtime because after 1pm he was neither use nor ornament.

When two of his regional companies merged he called a meeting with his staff and told them he was going to make them all rich and asked each one in turn what they thought of the merger. Silvia eyed him with disgust. He was doing a great impression of Lord Charles, the inebriated ventriloquist dummy.
"Who was working him?" she thought to herself.

Everyone told him what a fantastic opportunity it was going to be, working in a new city. Little did they know that they weren't all on the list to move. They'd missed their opportunity to tell him some home truths. When he finally got to Silvia she was ready.

"With twice as many people in the building it would certainly be warmer," Silvia offered, referring to the old metal window frames that would not shut properly and let all the heat from the radiators seep out into the cold winter mornings and told him she looked forward to being rich.

"And how are you going to do that dear?" he mumbled.
"Well, you just said you are going to make us all rich!" Silvia exclaimed, surely he couldn't have forgotten in that short a space of time.
"So how are you going to do that?"

A top executive in a flap jumped in and grovelled that Silvia was with them all the way and it's just her little joke Mr. Ventriloquist Dummy, she doesn't mean anything by it.

But Silvia did mean something by it. How was she expected to learn anything off these tossers when they were brain dead and drunk? The only consolation was that due to the move the company would have to pay her 'travelling' expenses on the train for at least 12 months. At £1000 a year, that was a lot of money in 1986.

While negotiations continued for the forthcoming move the following January, Silvia continued her daily ritual as usual, waiting for news of how many out the 65 staff would make it to Manchester, she knew she was safe but only 25 of them were going. A lot of friends would be left behind, she would miss the camaraderie, but there were some people she would not miss, especially the drunks.

Silvia's first stop at arriving in work was the loo. She'd brush her hair and reapply her lipstick and on this occasion when she flushed the toilet she heard a strange clanking noise coming from the cistern. She raised the lid and found a half empty vodka bottle floating around in there keeping cool!
"Not very hygienic but then alcoholics aren't all that worried about germs are they?" she mused.

Silvia reported it to the office manager, who came to look for herself. As there were toilets on each floor she narrowed down the culprit to being on that particular floor - the 3rd - as an alchy wasn't going to travel far to conceal their drug, it needed to be close by so they could get to it quickly. Like a swift detective, the office manager deduced that there where some PR executives and their new secretary Mrs. Touchy Typist, working on that same floor along with the accounts department and it certainly wasn't going to be any of her ladies. So the finger was pointed at the new arrival, who had been gushing about what a wonderful husband she had.

A few days later Silvia arrived at work, dashed into the loo and found the said secretary locked in the toilet cubicle and the office manager had to climb over the top of the stall to release her. Mrs. Touchy Typist was promptly sacked, and her wonderful husband came to collect her, but the hierarchy remained, but not for long. For once they didn't protect one of their own.

"Was it because she was a woman?" Silvia thought, as all the others were men.

Karma surfaced again when Mr. Drunk & Disorderly was suddenly rushed into hospital for several weeks stay with kidney stones the size of cricket balls. Oddly enough that was his favourite sport. It was to be his demise as he then suffered several heart attacks and strokes and was unable to return to work. Silvia pitied his poor wife and kids. She would have to work twice as hard now to put her boys through University, unless Mr. Drunk & Disorderly had forgone the cost of the odd pint and whisky chaser to pay for Critical Illness insurance to cover the cost of his mortgage on his ivory tower in Oxton, but somehow Silvia didn't think so.

"Alcoholics rarely think of anyone but themselves," she summarised.

"You can't negotiate with a terrorist or an alcoholic".

She needed the new career, as this one was also dead.

By the end of the year the list of 25 was announced and to her surprise all the alcoholics were omitted. Paid off. The relief was immense. She held her yearly train pass in her hand after being talked out of driving and looked forward to the new beginning.

MANCHESTER CITY UNITED

It was the first working day of the New Year; she flashed her train ticket to the guard. The journey was going to take at least an hour on the slow train or 45 minutes on the express. She hoped she would make the express.

She'd got up that morning and jumped into the shower and was ready by 7.30am so she could cadge a lift off her dad to Lime Street Station. It was a 20-minute drive through the Mersey tunnel and out the other side through building traffic. If they timed it just right the traffic lights opposite the station would turn to red as they approached, so she could jump out and cross the road, leg it up the station steps before they changed to green. Once inside she needed to check which platform it was leaving from that day (as they changed frequently) and hot tail it up to the nearest carriage and jump on by 8.05am.

It used to work like clockwork, until one day when the lights didn't change so she had further to run. She got onto the platform just as the train started to move slowly forward. The guard saw her running and shouted, "Come on, luv! You can do it!"
It was like being in a movie, escaping from the Germans to cross the Swiss border and seeing a freight train, running alongside it until you could hurl yourself safely inside and freedom.

Silvia ran level with the door of the guard's van at the rear of the train, he stood aside so she could jump on and catch her breath. It was 20 minutes before she could talk and go and find a seat, by which time they had reached St. Helens, the first stop for the express before racing on towards Manchester.

The express was better, more comfortable with high back seats so she could put her head back and doze off if she needed to. The slow, stopper train had passengers nodding like a toy dog on the parcel shelf of a car.

Silvia found a seat facing forwards and watched as more people piled on at St. Helens and walked through every carriage until they found a seat. Out of the corner of her eye she spotted a rather delicious man doing the same, then disappearing out of sight.

"Things are looking up, on this dull January day," she thought to herself.

When the train arrived at Victoria she made her way to the bus stop outside to catch the city mini bus, which wound its way round the city centre streets, dropping off at major points near offices to save a 20 minute walk and finally arriving at her new office at 9.20am.

Silvia entered the reception and was shown to her desk, the Creative Director's secretary checked her watch.
"Is she timing me?" observed Silvia.

Everything was in place and ready for the 25 'newbies' who were making their way into work from Liverpool, but it wasn't a warm welcome. Silvia felt some resentment from these Mancunians as they had lost some of their friends to redundancy too, and the 'newbies' were taking their place. Silvia thought this a tad unfair as they had also lost 40 friends and were now having to traipse 30 miles to and from work every day, and they weren't as friendly as Liverpudlians. She'd just have to get used to the cool reception.

That night she began the marathon run again, no time to wait for a bus when it's 5.30pm and your train leaves in 18 minutes! If Silvia missed it it would be another 45 minutes until the next one. She removed her heels and put on her flat leather boots. As the clock hit 5.30pm her coat was on and she was out the door. She ran the full length of Cross Street and into Victoria Station, the train was bang on time but it was the stopper and she knew she was in for an uncomfortable hour-long journey.

Silvia struggled to keep her eyes open. The gentle rocking of the train sent most passengers off into a deep sleep. She heard some girls giggling and looked up. They were staring at a poor fella who was in the process of nodding off but couldn't manage to keep his head upright. It rolled from sided to side with the lurch of the train over the tracks and his eyes were desperately trying to stay open in case he missed his stop. His mouth was gaping and he began to slide down the leather seat, his legs splayed out in front of him, but he was blissfully unaware that he was being watched.

An hour later they arrived in Lime Street, then it was a mad dash to the underground to catch a train on the Wirral line. If she took the West Kirby train she could get off at Moreton, but would have a 20 minute walk from the station or she could get off at Birkenhead Park and get a connecting bus that stopped right outside her house. The bus it was. It was already 6.45pm and the rest of the journey might take another 45 minutes if the connections were on time.

Silvia arrived home at 7.30, reheated the dinner her Mother had left her. It was in a frying pan on the stove covered in foil. She gently lifted it to see what delicacy laid therein – half cooked liver in a pan, congealed blood, cooked on the top and still raw underneath. Her stomach lurched like the train. There was no way she could eat this or she'd be sick again. So she tipped it in the bin outside and covered it up so her Mother wouldn't notice. She couldn't remember the amount of times she'd told her Mother to leave the raw ingredients in the fridge and she would cook it from fresh when she got home but it fell on deaf ears.

Silvia had to be careful, as she'd had food poisoning a few times before, once when she arrived home to find two pork chops under the grill to be reheated, which came out hard enough to resole her shoes. Once she was so ill that she missed work and got up to go to the bathroom only to bump into her Mother asking her what she was doing off work, and that there was nothing wrong with her and to get herself back in there! Munchausen by Proxy?

The next day Silvia missed the train home. "Bugger," she cursed, "Now I'll have to wait 45 minutes to until next one. With no book to read she looked around to see what would occupy her for that amount of time. There, sitting on the bench, waiting patiently, was the Gorgeous chap she'd spotted on the train the previous day. She sidled over and slid onto the other end.

"Did you miss it too?" she asked, hoping not to appear forward.

They chatted while they waited and discovered they were in the same line of business and he worked for one of her suppliers and that he'd often dropped things off at her old Liverpool office from time to time and sometimes the pub next door, if it was after closing time.

The train arrived and she half expected him to get in another carriage, but he didn't and sat with her all the way to St. Helens, chatting about their jobs. By the time he got off the train, Silvia was smitten. By the time she got home she was knackered. The train didn't arrive into Lime Street till 7.30 and by now the rush hour buses had stopped running, it was 8.30 by the time she walked through the door. Just enough time to have her dinner, yawn and go to bed!

It was starting to feel like she was living in a Guest House.

The next night, Gorgeous wasn't on the train, or the next day or the next and quite a few after that. Silvia was disappointed as it was the only thing that helped her pass the journey in a pleasurable way. She had a colleague who had migrated with her from Liverpool and she often caught the train with him, but he was prone to falling asleep due to the medication he was on.

She remembered one morning when she arrived in work and they asked her if she had seen him, she hadn't. Shortly afterwards he phoned the office to say he'd fallen asleep and woken up in Stalybridge, he'd completely missed his stop. Another time he'd fallen asleep and woken with a fright at his station, jumped up and ran off the train, only to leave all his artwork in the overhead luggage rack and ended up phoning the station at the end of the line to see if it was still there. One Christmas he did the same with a TV he had bought, got off without it, jumped back on to get it and as he was getting off again, he reversed through the doors only to have them close on the TV and the train started to move out of the station with him holding onto it and shouting for help. The train stopped and the doors fully opened but the TV crashed to the floor.

Victoria Station in Manchester was popular with TV crews filming period dramas. One morning Silvia had been to the dentist and caught a later train, only when she alighted in Manchester the platform signs had been changed to Gdansk and lots of soldiers in brown uniforms with red stripes round their caps were getting off too.
"That was a long sleep," Silvia quipped slightly worried that she'd woken in another time zone, until she realised her mistake.

Friday nights where popular for a drink after work and catching the last train home was always tricky. She had to keep one eye on the time and hopefully remember which pub she was in and time it so she could get to the station on time. One particular night she left it a bit too late and took a taxi with her friend, Nina.
"Don't worry," her friend told her, if you miss it we'll jump another cab to the next station see if we can beat it there."
She jumped out of the cab at the station, ran along the concourse to her platform and through the gate, suddenly finding herself running on tip toe across countless cables strewn across the floor. She felt like a footballer in training, stepping in and out of tyres. She ran onto the platform, saw the train still parked there and turned and shouted to her friend, "It's still here, see you Monday," and ran off.
All her friend heard was "CUT" by the director. Silvia had run right through a film set and didn't even notice.

It was several weeks before she saw Gorgeous again. He seemed to be pleased to see her again too. They chatted on the way home and when they got to his stop at St. Helens, he asked did she want a lift.

"I live on the Wirral," she told him.

"That's OK, I'm in no rush to get home,"

"Ok then," she smiled, and got off the train with him.

It was a long way from St. Helens, into Liverpool then through the tunnel to the Wirral and he wouldn't even come in for a drink, just dropped her off and returned home to Liverpool.

They saw each other nearly every day on the train then for the next 3 months until one day she received a phone call from him, asking her if she would like to go out for a drink after work. It was official, a first date.

They met at the station, and got off at St. Helens and he drove her to a little village pub in Rainhill. He told her of his plans to buy a house there, as it was easier for travelling to Manchester. He drove her to the one he had in mind to show her where he would like to eventually live and asked her if she could see herself driving down this leafy street every night.

"Nah," said Silvia, playing hard to get.

Nine months later they moved in together.

LIVING IN SIN

The house was quaint but it needed a lot of work doing to it. From the outside it was pretty as a picture, all black and white – almost Tudor style. It had a small front garden with a compact willow tree and a rockery.

"Hopefully the neighbours won't complain about it blocking their light," she informed Gorgeous, as he hadn't even considered it when house hunting.

The back garden was larger with a fish pond and real fish, overshadowed by bushes and shrubs to give shelter from the afternoon sun.

What a shock inside. The first thing Silvia noticed as she walked through the front door was the huge electric meter in the hallway that was stuck on the lower wall with no cover.

"That will have to have a cover on it," Silvia explained, "so we don't electrocute ourselves."

"Yes I fancy a nice, real wood piece to go over it," Gorgeous agreed.

The living room was beige - beige walls, paintwork and the carpets and curtains that they had taken with them had also been beige. Even the two venetian blinds they had left were beige. Silvia hated beige.

The dining room housed a bright red central heating pump, which had been concealed behind a piece of furniture, but was now blatantly on show.

The first thing that had to be changed was the kitchen; it was a long galley kitchen with one small radiator at the entrance and an ill-fitting window over the sink, which let in cold air through a one inch gap at the top, which she had to stuff with cotton wool to keep the draught out.

All the units were fastened to a wood panelled wall, which had been papered over with woodchip and painted a sickly yellow colour. When Silvia tapped them they sounded hollow and were found to be attached with batons to breeze-block – not plaster. The only upper unit itself held onto the wall with only one screw and fell down on Gorgeous's head when he unwound it.

They bought a new kitchen from a flat pack company and just about managed to get it into the car with one last shove of the worktops, which unfortunately hit the windscreen and cracked it.
"Bugger!" Gorgeous said, frustrated. Any saving they had made in the MFI sale now had to be used to replace that.

They stripped the kitchen and revealed the bare breeze-block underneath all the wood panelling. They levelled the floor from the badly built extension.
"No spirit level was used here," she thought to herself, and they spent the rest of the week building and fitting units, cooker, fridge/freezer and washing machine.

When Silvia arrived home on those wintery nights, the first thing she did was go into the kitchen and light all 4 rings on the cooker, turn on the gas fire in the living room, then go upstairs to change out of her work clothes. By the time she arrived back downstairs the rooms were nice and warm. She still needed to sort out a heater for their bedroom though, as although it had central heating the previous owners never bothered with a radiator in the Master bedroom.

The room didn't sit right either with the fitted wardrobes along one wall and the bed under the window. Some nights they had to sleep in bobble hats to keep the cold off their heads, as the inside of the windows would freeze up with condensation. There was no double glazing.

They surveyed the room to see what remedies could be done. They set about removing the central section of the wardrobes and put the bed in its place. It didn't cost them a penny and freed up lots of room for a chest of drawers, making it look more spacious. They bought a heater, which made the room more comfortable until they could afford to get a plumber to add an extra radiator in there and a bigger one in the kitchen.

The next main thing was the living room/diner. Silvia cashed in a savings policy and bought a carpet, measured up for curtains, and she fancied green, a nice fresh colour, but it wasn't fashionable in the shops so she had to wait for them to be made. The only coverings they had on the windows were the two beige venetian blinds to the front of the house and nothing on the back.

Strapped for cash, they had to budget carefully and wait until payday to buy anything else now they had the mortgage to pay, but at least they could sit on something with the second hand sofa they were given by Gorgeous's parents.

A meal out was out of the question, they needed all their cash for home improvements, so to entertain themselves Gorgeous taught Silvia how to play Backgammon.

"To make it interesting," he joked, "let's play strip Backgammon."

Silvia had never played before but with a few tips from Gorgeous he was soon sitting on the living room floor naked, and probably in full view of the neighbours who overlooked them from the back of the house, as Silvia was still waiting for the curtains to arrive.

They went in search of a cabinet to cover the hideous electric meter in the hallway and visited all sorts of shops and outlets and there just wasn't anything that fitted the bill. In desperation they walked into an Olde Worldy shop in the village and spotted a beautiful, double door cabinet, in marquetry wood. Silvia looked at the price.

"Wow, that's a bit expensive," she told Gorgeous, "and we'll have to take the back out of it to fit over the meter. I'm not sure we can afford this."

Gorgeous threw a wobbler, stamping his feet and waving his arms around like a frustrated, small child screaming, "I want real wood, I want real wood!"

Silvia relented with shock and they loaded it onto the back seat of the car. Once they arrived home Gorgeous proceeded to remove the backing and cut around the bottom edging strip to the shape of the skirting boards, so it would be a nice snug fit. Then he went very quiet.

"What the matter? Have you hurt yourself?" asked Silvia, concerned.

"No, it isn't real wood, it's veneer," he whispered to her, very quietly.

The bathroom refurb would have to wait until the summer, with only one loo in the house and money tight, it could be tricky with timings.

Work had improved, the Creative Director's secretary had left, so there was no one to check the time she arrived every morning so it made for a more relaxing atmosphere. Some of the Mancs had left too and others from nearby Preston and surrounding areas arrived, so Silvia was no longer the "newbie". They'd all moved on and so had her pay, which had increased to £11k a year. Not much but it paid the mortgage.

BLOWING A RIGHT HOOLEY

It was called the Great Storm and hit the south of England with magnificent force and although not officially classed as a Hurricane it was the nearest Britain had ever come to one.

On the night of October 15th 1987 there was a violent, extratropical cyclone moving in, that caused casualties in the UK and France as a severe depression with a 'sting jet' in the Bay of Biscay moved towards us killing 22 people. But it didn't only hit the south.

The first Silvia knew about it was that it was very windy outside and the huge 4x6ft quarter inch plate glass kitchen window was starting to bevel inwards. She could see her reflection like on the back of a convex spoon, expanding and shrinking again as the wind pushed forcefully against the glass. Something wasn't quite right.

She shouted to Gorgeous to come and have a look.
"Shit!" he exclaimed and ran outside into the garden shed to get some wooden sheets to hammer over the window for protection. He'd managed to get two pieces in place when there was an almighty pop and the plate glass window bevelled to its maximum, and then cracked from top to bottom.

Silvia ran outside to try and tell him what had happened, but the wind was so strong she couldn't hear her own voice shouting him, and neither could Gorgeous. He'd gone back into the shed to get another piece of wood and was unaware of the damage. Silvia couldn't even see him as the wind was blowing her eyelids shut with such force that they resembled a dog's cheeks flapping about in the breeze when it sticks its head out of a travelling car window.

Gorgeous emerged from the shed with the final piece of wood and nearly took off. It acted like a parachute catching the force of the wind. He fought his way towards the window and hammered it quickly into place to prevent it blowing in altogether and they both ran back into the house for safety. They could hear their carport roof rattling like Rolf Harris's wobble board.

The next morning, they surveyed the damage. Apart from the broken kitchen window, the side window had been dislodged from its position leaving a two-inch gap at the top, the cotton wool being completely sucked out. Sections of the carport roof had blown off and landed in various adjoining neighbours gardens.

They contacted their insurance company who offered them the money to get the windows replaced and pronto as winter was approaching. "We might as well get them all replaced," Silvia said, "at least it will make it warmer, the central heating system is struggling to reach a decent temperature."

"Yep," replied Gorgeous, "lets get those extra radiators sorted too and make it nice and cosy for winter."

"It's a good job we've got the curtains up to help keep the heat in, but that bloody Baxi back boiler in the chimney breast wakes me up every morning with a big 'whoosh' as the gas ignites, drives me insane but we can't afford to change that yet as the fire is like a blow torch and the only thing that helps keep the room warm."

With no savings left they applied for a loan, an expense they didn't really want but had no choice. It would take them 5 years to pay it off according to the calculations, but the temperature in the kitchen went up by about 20 degrees!

The bathroom refurb would definitely have to wait another year now.

IMMACULATE CONTRAPTION

They had registered with a local doctor and Silvia attended their contraception clinic. There were plenty of alternatives to the pill on offer and she needed to know what was best for her. The Gyny asked her what sheaths she preferred to use. It was like choosing a fashion accessary. She gave Silvia a range to try.

She arrived home with a bag full to the brim, tucked under her chin; all she needed was a cabbage and a cracker-jack pencil.
"What are those?" Gorgeous enquired, peering into the bag.
"3 months supply," Silvia replied with a cheeky grin.
"Looks like they'll last us 3 years!" he said and wasn't joking.

Every time they found the time to try one out, with their busy work lives and family visiting, the bloody phone would ring and coitus interuptus would ensue. The moment was gone. By the time they got down to the last few packs, they had to check the shag by dates!

The lack of intimacy came as a bit of shock to Silvia, Gorgeous was half Italian, but apparently it was only the top half.

Work was becoming manic. Silvia had been promoted to an Assistant Account Executive, which meant processing all the jobs that came into the agency through the design studio and managing schedules to meet the press deadlines.

It was never a 9-5 job before but now it was more like a 'flying by the seat of our pants" job as she was informed by the studio manager. Timings were often short but not impossible, but when every job became an urgent job it put everyone under stress. The bickering and infighting often blew up into frayed tempers and everyone worked on a short fuse.

The Account Executives seemed to be unable to say no to a client and would never check with the production department if there was capacity. Freelancers were hired to take up the workload and the permanent staff were often asked to work into the night to finish projects, arriving into work the next day already exhausted before they even started.

Silvia could no longer rely on getting out of work on time to catch a train after arriving at the station platform to see her train waiting then hearing the announcement that her 7pm, train had been cancelled and the next one wasn't until 8pm, she knew she wouldn't get home till 9pm. She went to find a phone to call Gorgeous, to let him know she'd be late.

When she got back to the platform there was a crowd around the guard and a kerfuffle was in progress. It turned out that the train on the platform had not been cancelled and had set off as planned and left half a dozen people stranded. Most people went for a taxi but Silvia couldn't afford the cost of one for the 30-minute journey, so back she went to call Gorgeous again, who jumped in his car to drive to Manchester Victoria Station to collect her.

During that winter, they changed the train timetable and Silvia could no longer get a direct train home. The timetable now meant that she had to catch the Chester train and change platforms in Earlestown and wait for the train from Liverpool to arrive and change track to take them back towards Liverpool.

At least twice a week it was cancelled and there was no waiting room on the platform. One night she was so cold that she couldn't feel her legs, despite trying to stomp her feet to promote circulation or march up and down the platform in an effort to get warm. They had gone numb from the icy wind.

Some of the other passengers decided to go to the pub across the road and wait for the next train. Silvia rang Gorgeous to tell him she'd be late again. She had a quick drink while one at a time they each took it in turns to peer outside and up the platform to see if the train was coming. On spotting it they shouted "train coming" and all drinks would be downed in one and a mass stampede would follow out of the pub, across the road and over the footbridge and onto the platform, just in time to board the nice warm carriages.

Silvia was tired all the time. The stress of work and trying to constantly meet tight deadlines, and trying to get home to have some form of work/life balance was not working for her. She needed a car so she could be independent of public transport and the morons who gave out duff information.

Money was still tight with all the bills to pay, so she asked the bank for a loan and they gave her the princely sum of £1000. A friend in work was selling her Father's car for £800 and the insurance was £200. She bought it, as it was the only one she could afford.

Now she was mobile, but embarrassed. The car was a Lada, an orange one.
Made in Russia and built for Russian winters, as she found out when the heater was almost instant on a frosty morning. 0-20 degrees in 6 seconds, almost. It was big and chunky and everything else on the road gave it a wide berth. Silvia christened it 'wobbly bob'.

Despite having another yearly pay increase, Silvia wondered if it was all worth it. Should she put up with all the stress as the money was good, but was quickly cancelled out with loans for the windows and the car, but at least they should both be paid off in 2 years **and** it paid the mortgage.

DON'T LET THE BASTARDS GRIND YOU DOWN

Silvia decided to get her marketing qualification. She was doing the job so thought she might as well get something tangible on her CV in case she moved on.

For three hours a night, two nights a week she toiled over books and thesis on how to comprehend that complicated thing that is the decision making process (just like trying to buy new shoes) and such informative procedures like how to sell a posh car to a monkey with money to burn.

Most of it was just common sense as she performed a lot of it on a day-to-day basis in her job. There were four modules she needed to pass to gain a certificate qualification and eight for the diploma. As the classes started at 6pm she needed to leave early to get to the college on time, but it was inevitable that that was never going to be easy. Her role meant she could rarely leave on time never mind early as she had deadlines to meet and unless she wanted holes to appear in the next day's newspapers, where an advertisement should have appeared, then she had to stay to make sure everything that needed sending was sent. The times Silvia dashed out of the door and legged it like a marathon runner to her car, only to find herself stuck in a traffic jam was too numerous to mention. She invariably arrived late to the courses to the dismay of the lecturer and sometimes even so late she'd miss the first 1.5 hours class altogether! So consequently the Economics module had to take a back seat.

One night she was in such a rush that in her haste to look behind to see what was coming Silvia failed to see that the car in front had stopped and she clipped the lady's bumper. After frantic swopping of phone numbers and insurance details she received a letter a few days later demanding compensation for whiplash.

"It was just a little bump, for goodness sake!" Silvia exclaimed, when she opened the letter. "I hope her next shit is a hedgehog! Hard and prickly."

Silvia could hear the production manager's voice in her head, "Don't let the bastards grind you down." He was a right comedian and one of the few people

that kept her going - the carrot dangling in front of the donkey.

Silvia passed three out of the four and was told she could resit the failed one again while studying for the next four subjects.

She signed up for the second year only to find that some of the syllabus she'd taken in the first year had become obsolete and all the sweat and aggravation it had taken her to memorize the formula for standard deviation (statistics) was now no longer applicable.

"Bugger," fumed Silvia.

She felt like the system was always trying to block her progress. Or was Fate trying to tell her not to move in this direction perhaps? She noticed, however, Economics was still on the bloody list.

Silvia recollected those immortal words that Dozy Dorian her stats teacher had been telling her for months, that it would suddenly click in her head and all would become clear. It became clear to Silvia that Dozy Dorian didn't have a clue how to teach statistics and spent the last three months of the course trying to swot at home from a book that luckily set everything out in easy-to-understand stages. It wasn't exactly Maths for dummies as this was the Chartered Institute of Marketing!

It was only on the insistence of the other members of the class that they had Dozy Dorian replaced (so it wasn't just her struggling) with a true professional who taught A-Level maths, who explained everything there was to know about statistics, precisely, straightforwardly, the laws of probability and the square root of all evil - although combining the two Silvia never won the lottery - but she amazed herself with an 'A' level pass grade C. She was still glad she had passed this one as it was Maths, and Silvia loved Maths.

BEER FESTIVAL

Silvia needed a break from work and study and when her friend mentioned a real ale beer festival up in Durham, she jumped at the chance to get away for the weekend.

The gang had booked to go up on the coach so they could have a few beers on the way. Silvia and Gorgeous didn't drink much just the odd cider or glass of wine, but thought it would be nice to see another city for a change.

They were all loaded onto the coach and set off for the 3-hour journey and Gorgeous took a Travel Cap sickness tablet to stop him feeling sick on the journey or worse.

A rather odd looking chap boarded and settled himself in seat 52, back row, huddled into the corner. Odd because his hair looked plastic, resembling the likes of Betty Boo or a plastic Ken wig with a green tinge to it. The gang eyed him with suspicion.
"Maybe he's overdone it with the Brylcreem," Silvia acknowledged to her friends.
"We'll christen him Travel Cap," said Belinda, and ring-pulled a can.

The journey went without hic-cups and they arrived at their hotel, ditched their bags and went out on a tour of the town, market square, over cobbled streets and bridges, through narrow alleyways which led to the street higher up and after a few tipples in the local pubs they set off down steps on the Elvet Bridge to the Prince Bishop boat tour along the river.

The boat passed along the rear of hotels and open fields with people fishing and offering great views of the Cathedral and Castle. Some on board were a bit worse for wear and for a laugh thought it was funny to do a 'mooney' to the guests of the hotel on the way back, but from the distance involved not many lifted their heads from their newspapers and books.

That evening there was fun and laughter at the Beer Festival with people being sponsored to sit in a cold tub of beans for charity, a jazz band playing music early on and a rock band later. Some students came in soaking wet and smelling of smoke.
"Blimey, you two stink of smoked fish," she informed them.
"We fell in the river and lit a fire to get dry," they proudly announced.
Silvia hoped they would do better in their exams.

Silvia and Gorgeous amused themselves by drinking the cider and perry on offer and by the time he had only drunk 2.5 glasses of the stuff he was blurry-eyed. They watched people going into the strong room, where the ales were more like Guinness and Porter, and coming out the other end with blood shot eyes and giggled to each other.

After the dancing had finished and the music had stopped they needed food and there was plenty on offer in a student town. Too late for a Chinese or Indian, they settled for Kebabs at midnight, all grease and sauce running down their arms as they tried to hold the huge parcel in both hands long enough to take a bite. Fine cuisine.

Breakfast the next morning was the full English and plenty of tea to wash away the greasiness left over from the previous night's kebab before further exploration of the town's shops.

It was Saturday and the morning market was in full swing with stalls inside and out and some lovely unusual novelty shops and cafes tucked away.

Silvia still had to be careful with her money and was aware of the temptation to buy trinkets that would sit on shelves gathering dust, forgotten until eventually they would end up in the charity bag. So she restrained herself and only bought essentials or things she knew she would get a lot of use out of. The first stop was M&S; she desperately needed a new bra, as the underwire from the one she was wearing had worked its way out of its position and was now manoeuvring itself up between her cleavage and popping out the top of her T-shirt. She looked like the Stasi Secret Police had her wired.

They meandered over ancient bridges to the next part of the town and found a Chinese restaurant along the riverbank that served tea with a chrysanthemum flower in it, which opened slowly like a time-lapse film and floated to the top. Silvia was mesmerised. Gorgeous was more interested in how much food he could eat on the menu. She christened him "the bottomless pit" because he could eat and eat and eat and never put any weight on. He was constantly hungry. Silvia's Mother had told her that she would rather feed him for a week than a fortnight.

The town was pretty in the old part and more modern in the new area they had extended to, on the other side of the river, and the atmosphere in the Beer Festival so friendly that they decided to make it an annual event, somewhere they could go to relax and soak up the atmosphere, have some time on their own as well as with their friends, enjoy a nice meal and stay in a peacefully quiet hotel, and chill.

That night at the Beer Festival was as good as the first one, they took the cider, their friends tried the beers, the band played on and the locals got up close and personal and Silvia was always amazed how people could fall asleep on a barstool and remain upright. When one of their group did this they placed a sign over his glasses saying 'closed'.

While they were all sitting on the edge of the stage between sets, Silvia heard a guy mention something to his mate about a young woman standing in front of him.
"I'd like to get into her knickers," he said.
Overhearing him she replied, "Forget it, there's already one arsehole in there."

The quick wittedness of her answer had everyone showering beer from their lips in raucous laughter.

The last day they all decided to hire a boat and go down the river. The boys took the oars and began their rhythmic rowing in silence. Silvia spotted a sign along the bank saying 'weir' and knew they should turn back.
"Weir'" she pointed to the sign and informed them they needed to turn round.
They ignored her like they were in some sort of trance.
"Weir," she told them again.
Nothing.
"Weir!!" she screamed, this time panicking as she wasn't a great swimmer and didn't want to end up smelling of smoked fish like the students. "We need to turn back!"
It was until she muttered some expletives to Gorgeous that the boys suddenly 'woke up' and turned the boat around.

COUNTRY BUMPKIN – MACCLESFIELD

Silvia was knocked out again when her office decided to relocate to a tiny hamlet in the Cheshire countryside, four miles outside the nearest town, and it would take an hour each way to drive there and back again. She was not a country girl. Silvia liked a bit of noise and buses and trains - except when she was trying to sleep - a bit of hustle and bustle to show there was life around. All she could see out of the windows were trees blocking the view.

The building itself was a beautiful listed mill house with a basement. Her office was in the servant's quarters in the attic with a small fireplace that housed a swarm of wasps in the summer and let in the howling gales in the winter. The two windows were but small slats - the likes of which Robin Hood and his merry men might have taken aim from - but as she didn't own a bow and arrow, totally useless in letting in any daylight only more wasps.

Silvia missed the town centre shopping with all the big stores she could peruse during lunchtimes, where she could buy her clothes and make up, but did benefit from free car parking which saved her £1000 a year and she was now earning £12k a year - a lot of money in 1992. The nearest supermarket was just down the road from the office so she could at least get some supplies in for dinner on her way home and let the traffic (and the mad dash idiots) die down before she hit the motorway.

She missed being able to meet friends in town after work for a meal and have the luxury of getting the train if she wanted a drink, but here it would have taken hours to get two trains home again.

To save herself some 'getting ready for work' time, Silvia decided she needed a drastic haircut. She booked herself into the salon one Saturday morning.
Sharon asked, "So how are we wanting it today?"
Silvia replied, "Short back and sides."
Sharon was horrified, she'd been taming Silvia's long hair for years, teasing it into shape with layered cuts and tinting it with the latest colour trend.
"Are you sure?" she exclaimed, slightly grief stricken.
"Of course. I have some old colour still growing out and I'm fed up of trying to control it. It's starting to look shabby and unkempt. So cut it all off. At least them I can wash it every day or rub it over with a wet flannel and it will be dry in seconds.

So Sharon clipped away as Silvia's long tresses fell to the floor. By the time her hair was dried and styled it looked like a motorcycle crash helmet. It reminded her of a joke "Put your crash helmet on tonight love, your going through the headboard!"

Sharon showed her the finished look in a mirror so she could see the back. Silvia never said a word, paid and left. Stepping outside, people began to stare. Silvia wasn't sure if they were staring because they liked or hated it, or thought she was an alien from another planet, but knew as soon as she got home she would put her head straight into the sink and rewash it, then leave it to dry naturally.

The result was amazing, her auburn hair turned into soft curls as it dried and formed a short bob shape. It was perfect.

Silvia shared the office with some posh totty, all designer suit and gold buttons. In fact the whole building was full of clones of her in varying degrees of snobbery, well this was the Cheshire countryside, darling, and the poor souls didn't get out much, except to expensive dinner parties, and still left their cars and houses unlocked at night thinking that no one would dare intrude upon them.

Everyone called each other by their full names Claudia, Felicia, Samantha - Silvia was glad her name also ended in an 'A' too, it was obviously a prerequisite for getting on with the 'in' crowd. If she'd still been in Liverpool they'd have been called Claw, Fel and Sam no bother, and whatever happened to good old names like Tracy, Sharon and Debbie?

One day Silvia horrified Fake Fel, who's Father was minted, lived in Brussels, worked for the Government, held cocktail parties for dignitaries and paid a fortune for the re-run of his daughter's wedding because it rained on the day and she refused to smile.

Here was a woman who bought her Mother a scarf from Marks and Sparks, and it was rumoured that she had cut out the label and replaced it with a Hermes label from her own scarf. Like Mummy wouldn't notice, poor thing.

Here was a woman who'd admired a scarf of Silvia's. Hand outstretched to touch the fabric whilst asking, "Is it silk?" Silvia informed her that it was indeed 100% polyester. She retracted her hand as if stung by one of those pesky wasps and reviled in the horror that she'd almost touched it.

Here was a woman, a director of the company, who spent a fortune on her clothes and still managed to look like a plain Jane when she turned up at the Christmas do in a black skirt and baby pink blouse (which apparently cost her £400). And here was a woman who believed in keeping her assistants down. She had poor Claw running round like a mad woman while she sat in her office all day reading life-style magazines and took all the credit.

Silvia soon discovered that all the directors were like that. They operated a clear desk policy - which meant "give everything to my assistant to deal with because I really can't be bothered anymore. I just want to sit here on my skinny ass and earn a fat salary while I charge my Sainsbury's shopping bill to my expense account as home entertaining of clients".

Sam demanded that she see all of Silvia's clients when they paid a visit to the agency. Unfortunately, one of them had other ideas. He'd sneak in under a cloak of secrecy, have the quickest meeting known to man and be out the door again faster than a fireman sliding down a greasy pole before Sam had chance to run down two flights of stairs to catch him. Silvia was hauled over the tiles.

It was a race to the MD's office to explain herself, but Silvia was at a disadvantage being in the attic, Sam was on the floor below and won hands down when she slammed the door of his office in Silvia's face. No amount of explanation that the client had requested not to include Sam would suffice. Silvia knew she was on a losing streak; not getting the back up she deserved and felt like she was wandering around in a maze with no exit in sight.

With all this shit going on and trying to leave at a decent time to get to night classes - an hours drive away now - it was inevitable that Silvia would miss some important lessons. "Law and Finance are two things you just can't learn on your own!" she fretted.

It was taking over an hour each way to drive to and from work, coupled with the fact that after eight months of slogging it over the Thelwall Viaduct, right in the middle of all its major rebuild works and exit 19 on the M6 being the most choked up by accidents, Silvia decided to sod it and find another job.

Filled with despondency that the system she'd help pay for had once again failed her but with a few more qualifications under her belt she turned right at the crossroads, took her last earful of bullshit and bogged off on another route, failing to understand, yet again, the insanity of the world around her, enveloping her, crushing her, drowning her with utter disbelief and despair. There must be SANCTUARY somewhere, but where?

A long time friend and one of her migrating colleagues from Manchester decided he'd had enough at the same time and decided to move back to Manchester after winning two prestigious accounts and set up on his own. Four months later he was established enough to take Silvia on board. It isn't what you know it's whom you know that counts.

But a small firm meant less hands to the pump and Silvia found herself struggling, yet again, to meet those deadlines and get to those night classes and after another year and only three passes out of four exams Silvia decided to cut her losses. It was work that paid her mortgage not the education system. From now on knowledge will mean sitting at home reading the books or learning from a mentor.

Silvia's salary increased again.

Well it paid the mortgage.

CHRISTMAS IN CANCUN

They planned a holiday to celebrate their 10-year anniversary, in the hope that they could relax enough to enjoy each other again and decided to do something they'd never envisaged before – a Christmas and New Year break.

They informed their families that they'd celebrate Christmas a week earlier this year as they were going to Mexico. Everyone on Gorgeous's side of the family was in full support and said they wished they could do the same thing. The last person Silvia thought would ever complain would be her Mother, but she did. "But Christmas is for families," she said, miffed.

They booked anyway and prepared themselves for a 10-hour flight. Once they had checked in they were informed that there was a four hour delay so they needed something to occupy them while they waited and were reduced to spotting mature ladies wearing lurex flatties with matching shoppers to take on board.

After the 10 hour flight Silvia had segs on her bum and eyes like road maps, her seatbelt didn't fit anymore with the swelling and after watching two movies she'd already seen her ears were sore from shoving ear plugs in them and trying to keep them there.

On arriving in the Mexican airport building there were 2 forms to fill in, one for passport control and one for customs to get your luggage through without declaring anything. For this last one Silvia had to decide for herself if she did or didn't have anything to declare and press a button on a traffic light system to get through.

At last they arrived at their All-Inclusive in Cancun. They had been up for 21 hours and were in desperate need of a kip. After signing another form for the room key, safe key and TV remote control they were fitted with luminous pink wristbands - which clashed with everything Silvia had brought with her for the trip, except black – and told not to remove them for the next two weeks. Once the snapper had been closed together that was it, handcuffed, and everyone knew which hotel you were from.

They'd paid £1500 each and the hotel room still smelt musty, just like when you go to Spain or Greece at the beginning of the season. The sofa was torn and the curtains had dirty stains on them. Their initial disappointment improved greatly when Silvia switched off the air-conditioning - which rumbled away to its heart's content – and all fell quiet and the smell disappeared too.
The view from the balcony was amazing, overlooking gardens and the Caribbean Sea.

They dumped the cases and headed for the dining room. More disappointment. It never ceased to amaze Silvia that people could spend so much on a holiday and spend the whole time in a shell suit. The bar was full of them. The Germans had appeared to have taken over Scousers in this particular fashion trend.

At least the food was nice and the beer free but jet lag was beginning to rear its head, so time for bed, said Zebedee.

Gorgeous likes a flat pillow and Silvia likes a big one, between them they interchanged and tested various combinations from the four that had been supplied but the only thing that worked for Silvia was placing a folded towel from the bathroom under hers which bulked it up a bit, but Gorgeous had nightmares all night on his and every time he tried to snuggle up to Silvia his wristband scraped across her skin waking her up with a sharp jolt.

She could just make out her Mother's voice, "It's the best form of contraception." Just like she did at one family party when Gorgeous had an upset stomach so she plied him with a mixture of Stone's Ginger Wine and Port. Ten minutes later he was unconscious in bed. "Thanks mum," said Silvia, so she stayed up till 5.30am with her friends instead.

The next morning their holiday rep informed them they were in for a few cloudy days but on the third day it was forecast to be hotter than a chilli pepper. They decided to do a recce of the resort and get their bearings.

Chosen by a computer as an ideal, would-be holiday resort, the Mexican government quickly set to work to clear the vast jungle that once covered this L-shaped island. Construction work uncovered hundreds of snake pits and so they gave the resort the name of Cancun, meaning snake pit. They were hoping to attract Americans and Canadians and particularly the 'snowbirds' who fly south to warmer climes for the winter.

A single road runs the length of this varied resort, lined with smart hotels, restaurants and bars, not to mention the odd shopping mall with jewellers stocking more silver than Long John's den, Cancun soon attracted the attention of over one million tourists a year, which has risen to over six million.

With the Caribbean Sea on one side and the Nicupte lagoon on the other - complete with lush mangrove swamps and talcum powder sand – it was easy to see the attraction and no matter which side of the road you are on it's always beachside.

If you liked sports then this was the place to be. When there's a breeze blowing, wind surfers shoot past faster than Speedy Gonzales! A jogging path, which was safe to walk along even at night, served the whole area and there were little booths every so often hiring out roller blades. Silvia's balance wasn't good with anything that moved under her feet, but hey she was on holiday so anything could happen – even sex!

If that's too energetic a few pesos get you a bus ride (and there's one every few minutes) from one end to the other. The area is divided into 4 zones ABCD and a taxi will charge you one price to go into each zone. It may cost ten times the amount of the bus, but that's still only a few quid.

It couldn't be easier to find your way around. Distance is measured in kilometres from the centre of downtown Cancun right through the Hotel Zone. Our hotel was at 4Km and Planet Hollywood at 14Km. Most restaurants, shopping malls, bars and discos give this measurement as part of their address, so it was easy to see how far they had to walk back from their recce.

They strolled along Kukulcan Boulevard and hotel after hotel with the odd Shopping Mall for the souvenir hunter thrown in here and there, and all would be revealed that evening as they had booked a bar crawl night with Karaoke and Disco.

The hotel reps put on trips to different bars each night with free drinks thrown in for good measure. Senor Frogs is hopping, the walls and ceilings covered in luminous slogans, one read 'More marriages break up through dishonesty rather than infidelity!'

A free ice-cold Corona beer was given to them at the door. A water slide from the balcony lead to the lagoon outside and at regular intervals the Tequila Conga sprang up, pouring a shot in your mouth as it passed from a great height. After 2 rounds it was time to move on, the luminous signs were beginning to merge into one!

Next stop Guadalajara with its Mariachi band and free Margaritas. Fat Tuesdays was a free jelly cube laced with Tequila and a Bucking

Broncho, all make for a head spinning night. Of course Silvia didn't drink much so refrained from most offerings as it wasn't compulsory.

The final stop was Boom nightclub and it wasn't fashionable to be seen there before midnight. By the time they arrived it was heaving, two rooms playing middle of the road music and the other pure waving your arms above your head dance music, each track pounding with the same steady beat and lasting about 15 minutes.

They survived until 1.30 until Silvia's feet started to ache in her heels and like Cinderella she knew she had to get back to the hotel and remove the damn things.

By the following morning the sun was out in force and they made the most of spending the day by the pool, but by 6pm they were so tired from the previous night that they decided to go and have a sleep before dinner. When Silvia woke up it was dark, "It must be about 8pm," she thought and looked over at Gorgeous, who was still in a deep sleep. She took her watch to the bathroom so not to disturb him with the light on. It was 2am; they had slept for 8 hours! The long distance travel, the delay at the airport, the late night party and the 30 degree Celsius heat had all taken its toll on them.

"Too late for dinner, now," Silvia mused and got back into bed. By 6am she was wide awake but Gorgeous was still fast asleep. She couldn't sleep anymore so took a shower and got ready for an early breakfast. By the time she was ready Gorgeous had woken and did the same. He enjoyed his food and hadn't eaten since his burger snack at 4pm the previous day, even though they were on an all-inclusive holiday. When they arrived at the dining room at 7am, the rope was still across the entrance and there was a queue of people all in their shell suits waiting to go in. Silvia felt disappointed and overdressed, she had brought lots of nice dresses with her to wear, ones she didn't get chance to in the UK because the summer weather was never that good.

That morning they decided it would be best to just take it easy by the pool again as they didn't want to miss another night. All the Brits they had met in the past few days were pleased to see them and enquired what had happened to them the previous night. Silvia regaled them with the tale. They in turn told her of disgruntled rumblings being heard from some of the clientele - this was missing, that was missing, all the sports facilities that had been promised were not available, only one ping pong ball was available, all the bicycles were broken, and complaining that the only entertainment on Christmas Eve was to book into the restaurant early to ensure you got a place for the special meal being cooked by the chef, otherwise it was the buffet, and generally about the standard of the hotel.

Silvia had been too tired to notice and so was quite happy. She had a quiet room with a sea view from the balcony and was able to sleep at night with the air-con off and the black out curtains – obviously. The food was good, there was a beach terrace and bar and the restaurant bar was open till 9.30pm, when the upstairs bar opened. The Mexican restaurant at the front of the hotel offered a five-course menu all included in their package and the wine had a kick like a mule.

The only disappointment for Silvia was the evening entertainment, it was always geared up for the kids early on and the adult entertainment didn't start until much later when everyone was drunk and about to fall asleep.

Most of them were complaining that the bars weren't well stocked but as Silvia wasn't a big drinker it was good enough for her, "I mean how many tequilas can you swallow in one night?" she asked. One lady they had met had been over the road to a four star hotel and was demanding to be moved. So when the anarchy gathered speed, collecting debris like a twister and heading for reception the poor holiday rep took the brunt of the vortex, with a whirling mass surrounding him. He had no choice if he wanted to get out alive, he was going to have to implode the situation, so after some hasty phone calls they were offered a move to their sister hotel across the road, they gladly accepted.

Silvia and Gorgeous were a bit sad at all the chaos and that they wouldn't see their friends again and went back to their room for a rest before dinner. The phone rang. It was reception offering to move them too, at no extra charge. Silvia had had a choice of two hotels in the brochure both 3* PLUS, both the same price and facilities, so she picked the one with the best looking pictures of the hotel.

"I'd like to see the other hotel first," Silvia informed the management and it was arranged that they could pop over and take a look. What they saw amazed them, it was Christmas Eve in true style, so they went straight back to the hotel, packed their bags and checked into their new hotel all in an hour.
She was amazed at how wrong brochure descriptions could be.

***

Their new room was smaller than the last one, but overlooked a man-made lake. They got ready for dinner and Silvia could actually wear a nice dress without being stared at because she wasn't wearing a shell suit.

The new resort had two restaurants and two swimming pools and looked like a beautiful white washed Mexican village, with a central plaza all set out for dinner with Champagne for 500 in the open air and everywhere was decorated with fairy lights, water fountains and party hats. The black gowns and gold shoes were out in force. The other holidaymakers wore tinsel necklaces and their best party frocks and the warm evening air mingled with the scent of bougainvillea. There was even a Nativity scene. This was Christmas in Cancun.

The hotel put on such a wonderful meal for everyone with music and dancing, and breakfast on Christmas morning was a late affair so they could all recover and not miss out. Silvia called home to wish her parents a happy Christmas. Her Father answered and informed her that mum was in bed with flu, so they wouldn't be having any Christmas Dinner after all.

They were also now on the lagoon side and the hotel had arranged a casual BBQ that evening on the beach. When Silvia walked onto the sand from the hotel landscaping she was greeted with a beautiful paddle boat, all lit up with fairy lights, sailing past. "Wow, how romantic. I'm so glad we moved," she said to Gorgeous. "Me too," he said.

The Yucatan Peninsula turned out to be a great place for the intrepid explorer, scattered with ancient Mayan ruins, like Tulum, Coba, El Ray and the most famous being Chichen Itza – which they had booked a trip to later that week, and their friends who had been the week before gave Silvia a tip. "When you get to the top, sit down and come back down on your bum," she informed Silvia.

They had to get up early for this trip and Silvia was always worried she'd sleep through the alarm but some hearty Germans woke her at 6am singing their hearts out, "They've obviously found the 24 hour bar," she thanked them, as she watched them walking sideways back to their rooms.

It was a four-hour trek on a coach in a straight line on a bouncy road, which was obviously built in a hurry and never flattened properly. Chichen Itza was built by ancient Mayans, nobody knew why or how as very little bones or work tools have ever been uncovered but their guide pointed out several mounds of rubble which the archaeologists had said were saunas, jacuzzis and an observatory for watching for any astronomical changes, implying that they may have been from "outer space" as they had mysteriously disappeared without trace.

It seemed a bit absurd to Silvia but the climb to the top of the "Castillo" or Castle was no mean feat and confirmed the phenomenon to her. She ascended on all fours, like Spiderman, refusing to look down until she'd reached the top. She thought she wasn't scared of heights until that moment, after 91 steps - all about one foot high and no hand rail, Silvia turned to face the scenery and so did her stomach.

All around was jungle; was she in Jurassic Park? A light aircraft took off out of nowhere, the jungle so thick you couldn't see the runway. It was so beautiful and secluded and she understood why they had chosen that spot. There was only one way down.

Other climbers were standing with their backs against the wall but with no barrier between her and a 91-foot drop Silvia couldn't even stand up. She shuffled her bum backward towards the wall and sat cross-legged unable to move. High Anxiety set in, combined with a banging headache.

God had kindly sent some clouds over before the climb to reduce the temperature slightly. Gorgeous offered her a nurofen and a swig of water and within a few minutes she was ready to descend, one at a time, on her bum whilst clasping a chain they had clamped down the middle of the flight of steps. Only when she reached the bottom 10 steps could she allow herself to stand up.

Silvia collapsed onto the surround grass to regain her composure, while Gorgeous decided to run back up the steps again and run back down. "How the hell can he do that?" she pondered, "he's fit as a butcher's dog." They were glad they had done it as they were amongst the last people to climb that fantastic monument due to its closure in 1997.

The next day Silvia could hardly walk. The muscles above her knees were aching. They had obviously not been used for a while, something she'd have to rectify when she got home. Her body was beginning to feel all-inclusive even though she was up early every morning and in the pool by 9.30am, swimming from breadth to length and length to breadth in 'square' circles.

They'd both been working so hard all year so this was a totally 'go at your own pace, no deadlines to meet, who cares if you sleep in, where's the fire?' holiday. They were going to relax, see some culture, try some sports and they might even have sex.

PARADISE

Xcaret, a natural lagoon theme park, a stroll through authentic jungle, explore botanical gardens, swim in underground rivers (life jacket compulsory), snorkel in the lagoon, and sunbathe in hammocks by turquoise streams. There's butterflies, turtles and wild birds hatching, mushrooms growing - the likes Silvia had never seen on her breakfast plate - and an aquarium where you can touch the flora and fauna.

Gorgeous had chosen to go for the underground swim but Silvia didn't like deep water and needed to be able to stop and put her feet on the ground. They were also warned that it could be claustrophobic down there but with exits every few hundred yards if you needed to get out it was also quite safe. The tunnel was 550 metres long so it's quite a swim, opening into lagoons with hammocks so you can get out and rest if you needed to.

It was good to have some time apart, as most couples just end up arguing with each other (much to the amusement of the other guests) because they aren't used to spending 24 hours a day in each other's company, and when they meet up again they have some interesting things to talk to each other about.

Silvia remembered a distant wine tasting holiday in France. One man ended up with a black eye having made advances to someone else's wife and the whole hotel got to know about it. "That's why careful planning is needed to ensure you choose a place with enough interests to occupy you both during the day, so you can enjoy your nights too," Silvia agreed with herself. "At least we'll have something interesting to talk about when we meet up again."

Silvia wasn't a sporty person. Her ideal holiday was relaxing by the pool and taking the occasional swim to cook down, a trip out to a place of interest, nice food, drink with friends they'd met but with no pressure to participate in anything if she didn't want to. Gorgeous would die of boredom just lying by the pool every day, so they always chose somewhere with tennis, canoes, wet bikes and other sports facilities so he can go and play with the other kids whilst she read a book and topped up the tan in peace.

Sometimes Silvia humoured him and would join in with his pursuits and sometimes she would drag him along to a disco, where he would stand dumbfounded. "Just wave your arms and wiggle your hips at the same time," she'd shout to him over the music, and laugh as he gyrated around with his snake hips.

Gorgeous packed all his clothes and valuables into a sealed bag, which would be delivered back to him once he reached the other end and Silvia set off through the jungle.

Pathways took Silvia meandering through ancient Mayan villages, which felt a bit scary on her own, but once she realised that she was in a safe theme park her anxiety calmed and she began to enjoy herself.

A photographer's dream, shafts of sunlight beaming through thick jungle, but Silvia only had a small Olympic Trip so wasn't holding out any hope of it picking out what her eyes could see.

Later that day they had booked a swim with Dolphins and were given a photograph and video of the experience. It was the nicest photo she had ever had of Gorgeous and he was with another woman – Melissa, the Dolphin - they both had a smile of their faces and it brought a tear to Silvia's eyes. What a fabulous day it had been and there was just enough time left for a swim in the lagoon and sunbathe on a tropical Mayan beach before the long coach ride home.

They didn't remember much about the journey home. One minute they were getting on the coach and the next they were arriving at the hotel, having fallen asleep on each other's shoulders, slobbering like a pair of nodding dogs. How attractive.

Although Silvia loved the idea of the All-Inclusive holiday, serving buffet style meals where you can eat yourself silly, and 24 hour bars where you can drink yourself sober, cable TV, safe and air-conditioning in every room, a good range of sports activities and evening entertainment, you never needed to leave the confines of your complex, Silvia still liked to get out and about and see the surrounding areas and try the local food.

The wristband she was given on arrival, that ensured they didn't pay for anything was impossible to remove without scissors and kept getting stuck in her hair when showering, was a minor inconvenience when it's a holidaymaker's hassle-free heaven, but she still had to remember that once back home she would need to pay the bill before leaving a restaurant.

WET LETTUCE

The next day it was overcast but still warm enough to go for a long walk along the boulevard. They could see storm clouds in the distance but hoped they would have reached a bar before it hit.

A taxi drew up alongside them and beckoned them in. They indicated that they preferred to walk a bit, so he left. A few minutes later he was back again. Again they waved him on. Then all of a sudden the downpour started to drench them and within minutes their clothes were stuck tight to their bodies. They heard a noise behind them, it was the taxi driver beeping his horn, they jumped in looking like drowned rats. Smart these Mexicans; he'd got himself a fare.

The taxi dropped them off at a local bar and although it was still a humid 20 degrees Celsius outside it was freezing inside with the air-con. Their clothes felt like ice and wouldn't dry – if they'd been outside in a shelter they would have dried in minutes. They couldn't walk back out now, so settled at the bar for a drink looking like wet T-shirts competitors.

Unable to stand it any longer they headed to the door only to see that the storm had got worse and the tropical rain was beating down on the pavements. If they attempted to wait for a bus they'd get even more soaked so they stood inside the doorway until they saw one approaching and ran for it as it approached the stop.

WET BIKES AND WATERSPORTS

Silvia put on her lifejacket and mounted the wheelless, throbbing lifebuoy and clung tight hold of Gorgeous. The noise was chronic and the smell of fumes would be banned in any civilised country. It was Gorgeous's first attempt on a wet bike and Silvia was a nervous pillion rider.

Gorgeous was wobbly, his steering was wobbly, Silvia was wobbly and her bum was twitching as they lurched forward, from side to side over the bobbing waves from other riders. "This is a good waist exercise!"

shouted Silvia. "Not to mention the inner thigh squeeze!" trying to stay on.

One circuit of the lagoon and Silvia was begging to be dropped back off onto the sand so he could go off again and play. Silvia went for a swim.

Gorgeous booked a deep sea diving lesson and was told not to have any alcohol the night before and no fatty foods for breakfast (he loved his cooked breakfasts) on the day of the dive, so he just had fruit (not his favourite).

Silvia went along to the pool on the day of his dive where they loaded him up with the gear. Face mask, mouthpiece, breathing apparatus, flippers and a weighted belt round his middle. After 30 minutes of safety training his bum was twitching too now. He disappeared under the water for a practise but shot back to the surface spluttering for air. Several attempts later he just couldn't get the mouthpiece clear and kept taking in water. His Jacque Cousteau days were over.

Silvia tried water aerobics. A tanned instructor shouted instructions whilst everyone jogged on the spot, quite difficult to do in 5ft of water, when you're only 5ft.2". Then he jumped out onto the pool edge and Gorgeous said she'd only joined in because he had a King Edward potato shoved down the front of his trunks. "Ah jealousy," Silvia smirked to herself. The Mexican standoff.

After the session they took partners and gave each other a water massage on the neck, shoulders, back, head and face. Silvia drew the short straw and ended up with a girl much to Gorgeous's relief.

Silvia liked boat trips but Gorgeous suffered from seasickness and would take a tablet to go along with her. So they booked a short cruise over to the Isla de Mujeres, 40 minutes away, for a night of feasting and partying. They were given a frozen slushy while they waited to board in the evening heat. It went straight to Silvia's sinus and caused painful brain freeze. She had to use Gorgeous's warm hands on her face to defrost her nasal passages.

It was worth the trip just to see the compare. A Jay Leonard look-a-like, he had males from every continent up singing a song of their choice. Japan won, not surprising with their love of Karaoke.

Gorgeous got queasy on the way back so Silvia asked him to dance to take his mind off it, but he was unable to find his sea legs with the boat rocking from side to side. Unable to speak, he just shook his head and sat rigid as a poker.

The approaching coastline was lit up with millions of twinkling lights. It reminded Silvia of the film 'Sleeping with the enemy' where Julia Roberts knocks out one of the lights so she can see where to swim to. It looked quite beautiful but Gorgeous couldn't appreciate in his semi comatose state. She'd have to review his medication.

TERRE FERME

The next few days were filled with landlubber's pursuits, as Gorgeous needed something solid under his feet. We'd met a couple with a 12-year-old daughter who was a dab hand at Tennis so Gorgeous challenged her to a dual. Silvia told her to wup his ass. An hour later he returned sweating bullets and said he'd won by two games but she said she'd only let him win because it was too hot and she couldn't be bothered. Silvia called for a rematch on a cooler day.

There was beach volleyball, water volleyball, water polo, water basketball but they were all too energetic for Silvia so she turned over to baste the other side.

When the temperature got the better of them (it was now 35 degrees Celsius) the cinema seemed to be a good option. It was air-conditioned and 101 Dalmatians was showing in English with Spanish subtitles.

They sat amongst Mexican families, with babies' pushchairs lining the isles.

At the end of the movie there was a big cheer and applause for a most entertaining film – something unheard of at home.

The cinema was in a grand shopping mall containing hundreds of jewellery shops with mounds of shiny metal in their windows to entice you in. Duty free perfume outlets, T-shirt shops, souvenir stores with the odd Harley Davidson and Levi shop for the enthusiast.

Silvia bought her Mother a pair of earrings for her birthday on Epiphany and umpteen T-shirts for the other folks back home, which was standard fayre in her family. A bar of rock just won't do, unless it's from Blackpool.

NEW YEAR'S EVE

Cable TV and several phone calls home confirmed that the UK was under a foot of snow on New Year's Eve while they were basking in glorious sunshine.

The hotel was preparing a New Year's Eve party to remember with balloons galore, a sit down dinner just like Christmas Eve and an entertainment programme to welcome it in.

At 1am Captain Hook's Pirate Boat was setting sail for a party until 6am followed by a hangover breakfast. A few years ago Silvia might have gone for that option but it's a rare occasion these days she can keep her eyes open past 10.30pm.

The evening meal was wonderful, with party poppers to let in the New Year; everyone was up dancing to the band and enjoying themselves. They'd met some lovely people but it was nearly the end of the holiday with only a few days to go, but what a wonderful time it had been.

Silvia had been glad she'd paid for the best Malaria tablets to reduce the chance of side effects, and as Mexico is a 'B' zone you only had to take a mild one once a week, from the day before you arrive and four weeks after you return home, which is a hell of a lot better than risking malaria.

"I look juicy to a mosquito," Silvia told Gorgeous, "just like curry is my favourite food, I am a mosquito's favourite nibble." So along with Antisan cream and mozzy spray she took her tablet once a week, like a good girl.

ALL GUNS BLAZING AT THE PLANET

As a special treat for their last night they queued with the rest of the eager outside a famous American Food Restaurant. Mexican's dine late so it's best to be early.

Half an hour later they reached the door, half an hour later they reached the bar, half an hour later they reached the table and half an hour later they had to leave as Silvia had picked up a tummy bug and was feeling queasy. She knew she was going to be ill and needed to get back to the hotel room as soon as possible.

As standard procedure the Management Team circle the restaurant and ask at your table if everything was to your satisfaction. Silvia knew she hadn't enjoyed her meal because she was feeling unwell and nothing to do with the meal as bugs usually take 24 hours to raise their ugly heads, but their companions came out all guns blazing!

"We'd ordered blackened prawns – not available, so we ordered calamari instead – we got chicken!" they shouted.

Silvia had ordered a salad and got a bowl of lettuce her rabbits would have been ecstatic over, but not what she'd get in the UK, there would be all sorts of delicious things, like tomato and cucumber, sweetcorn, avocado, spring onions and beetroot. Her medium steak sandwich was rare and the only thing that was eaten was the chips.

They were offered a 50% reduction and stayed, but Silvia returned to her hotel to empty the contents of her stomach down the toilet and the sink at the same time.

She reflected on the meal, "Now they'd obviously got 4 out of 5 P's in their marketing mix correct. The right people, in the right place, with the right packaging, at the right price but the Product availability was paltry," she analysed. "Oh well home tomorrow, hope I'll be fit to fly."

At least this was one holiday that she wouldn't put weight on.

LIFE IS HARD AND THEN YOU DIE

"This would be a great job if it wasn't for the clients," Silvia mumbled. "Half of them want the impossible and the other half are brainless gits who wouldn't recognise a good idea if it came up to them and punched them in the chops."

Most of the time she enjoyed it. It gave her a great sense of achievement when a project was done and dusted. Having watched its conception and development and when it finally went out of the door to a happy client, she knew she'd done well but she never blew her own trumpet. She left that to the others.

Those who kissed the boss's ass and couldn't tell him enough how brilliant he was and how brilliant they were too, of course, and oh what a great team they make. They underestimated Silvia to the point where she began to underestimate herself. But Silvia had trained that many plonkers who went on to better jobs with better cars and better salaries that she was often disillusioned.
"How do they do it?" she'd ask in despair.
Then one day she realised that the bigger gobs they had, the louder they shouted and their prospective employer would be bullied into submission.

They say if you tell someone something often enough, they begin to believe it in the end. Just like men do when they play psychological warfare. They tell you you're in the wrong and you say OK, sorry. Silvia wouldn't stand for that. She'd learnt to see the signs and tell them where to go - usually beginning with an "F" and ending with an "F" and having something to do with sex and travel.

She lost count of how many times she had stood in for her managers, when they were unable to perform their tasks through alcoholism and drug abuse.

"We must work as a team," they told her.

"Some team", thought Silvia, "roughly translated it means you stay here and do my job for a pittance, I'm off to the pub (business lunch), golf (I meet lots of prospective clients on the course) seminar on global marketing (chance to get away for a quick bit of nookie with my secretary) and will collect my fat salary on my return. And if the wife calls tell her I'm in an important meeting and can't be disturbed".

The secretaries used her like an agony aunt. Every time the boss's door was shut for more than 10 minutes they'd swarm around Silvia talking redundancy and asking for advice. The trouble was Silvia never noticed these things she was always too busy working, head down, pushing on regardless, but once the ball started rolling Silvia's mind began to work overtime - unpaid as well - and the secretaries did the exact opposite to any advice she gave them anyway.

"Why do I bother," she moaned.

Her boss, Peeve, couldn't spell for toffee and would often get his words mixed up. He asked her to type a letter offering as new employee a 'renumeration' package.

"It's remuneration," Silvia corrected him.

Sometimes she would despair at his comments, requesting that the work experience girl wear designer clothes - on the £50 a week he was paying her! When an important client from a local football club was due in he asked Silvia to go into town and purchase some designer toiletries for the bathroom.

Silvia shot him that 'How dare you ask me, as if I haven't got enough on my plate with all my work and deadlines, can't you ask one of your less worked employees to go' look, with one nostril turned up like he'd fallen in a bucket of shit and come up smelling like he'd fallen in a bucket of shit.

"OK, I'll ask someone else," he relented.

He asked Fleur, his new sidekick, who was only too happy to fawn over him, and the whole office thought she secretly fancied him anyway. Off she trotted to a famous department store on Deansgate and came back with a sumptuous range of towels and handwash from a well-known designer range.

Peeve's meeting went quite until his client decided to visit to the bathroom on her way out, but not before she'd happened to mention that all their supporters were scallies who were prone to wearing a certain designer label - the same one that now occupied the loo and most of his own wardrobe.

His face took on a look of someone who had suddenly been stricken with a bad case of wind and was clenching his buttocks so as not to fart in her presence. Silvia could hear his heart descending into the pit of his stomach and his bowels creaking as his ring twitched to keep the air in. There was absolutely no way he could get to the bathroom before her to retrieve the offending items and one side of his face twitched into a half smile as he watched her enter and lock the door. Karma.

The poor soul had tried so hard to impress - just like Hyacinth Bucket - but as usual the shit hadn't hit the fan but landed smack, bang all over his face. And so it came to pass that the harder you try there's always someone ready to piss on your chips, and if you don't shout loud enough people will not notice you. If you sit with your head down, beavering away, you'll be left to rot in the same hell hole for all eternity, retire on a crap pension and wear the same woolley jumper for the next twenty years till you pop your clogs and no-one comes to the funeral because they've forgotten who you are. Or worse still you die at your desk and no one notices for five days until they think you've forgotten to wear your antiperspirant.

Silvia knew that in advertising terms you're only as good as your last job, if you cock up all your good work is forgotten and your reputation's out of the door as fast as shit off a shiny shovel.

It wasn't only her working life that things were exasperating Silvia, everywhere she turned she was being prohibited. From trying to buy clothes to paying the Littlewoods pools man, everyone seemed to have 'one on them' and everyone seemed reluctant to help. Silvia called them SPO's - Sales Prevention Officers. She had money she wanted to part with but nobody wanted to take it from her. Silvia thought that it must be her hormones finally caving in; surely they all can't be tossers.

Alas, the money was getting better and it paid the mortgage.

WHEN ARE WE GOING TO WIN?

Every Thursday for the last million years, Silvia had collected the pools syndicate money from all those employees who were dying to tell the boss where to shove his job. And every week she was asked the same old question - "When are we going to win?"
"If I could predict that, do you think I'd be working here you soft shite?" she'd answer.
Fumbling for change they'd reluctantly hand over anything from foreign coins to paper clips. Some of them would tell her to F-off.
"And that's exactly what I'll say to you when we win and you haven't paid and come looking for your share!" Silvia would retaliate.
They soon coughed up the dosh.

Why did she bother, week in week out, even on holidays all collected and paid for in advance just in case the inevitable happened while she was away and she'd forgotten to put them on. It would be just her luck to find out, like the lady in the local paper, that all your lottery numbers had come up on a Wednesday and you only do them on a Saturday!

It was the thought of having too much money to even begin to think about what you'd buy with it after you'd whispered those three little words in your boss's ear, "stuff your job", that kept her going. The proverbial carrot in front of the donkey.

Silvia's friend Belinda said she wouldn't give up her job, she'd keep working until she had time to think about what to do with the money if she won.

"Stuff that for a game of soldiers! I don't have time to think in work. I'd be off on the QE2 while I thought about what I'd do with it," explained Silvia.

"Good point," agreed Belinda.

So it came as a complete shock when she handed over her £5.95 stake to her pools collector, who lived next door, what came next. To lighten her purse Silvia gave him all her slummy, which she'd often done in the past, as opposed to a cheque for such a meagre amount. It must have been all that copper and silver affecting his brain but the ensuing argument resulted in Silvia being so incensed that she felt it necessary to write to Littlewoods to complain:

Dear Sir/Madam,

I would like to make a formal complaint about the attitude of my pools coupon collector Cedric Shithead.

On Saturday afternoon, 22nd May, Mr. Shithead knocked on my front door and thrust a bag of coins in my face and shouted, "You see this, well I'm not having it!"

I apologised to Mr. Shithead for supplying the total sum in a mixture of coins, but at the time it was the only money I had on me. I told him I was sorry as I didn't realise he had to carry it around with him, at which he replied he didn't, he just takes it to the bank - in his car, and as he does a 'pools round' he must collect lots of change from people - which he denied, saying he gets very little change.

So I offered to change it back for him as it was three days later and I had a five-pound note, but he said he was going out to spend it. He also complained that I hadn't 'bagged it' for the bank, I thought you paid him to do this, and if he said if he took this into a shop on the high street they'd refuse to take it - but we both know that shops are always short of change and are glad of it, and to prove the point every shop I visited that afternoon were all glad to take my change.

Personally, I couldn't see what all the fuss was about as I have supplied him with coinage before and he's never complained. I even give him the coupon a day earlier every week at his request so as not to inconvenience him because he goes shopping on a Thursday. His wife Iris later informed me that her husband had had a word with his manager and asked him what he should do if he's handed coinage again in the future and his manager told him to refuse to accept it!

If this is standard practice for Littlewoods Pools then it isn't the competition from the Lottery that you need to worry about but your own collectors could be losing you money! Perhaps you should initiate some formal training on how to be pleasant to your customers because this is one customer you no longer have."

Yours faithfully,

Silvia Fernsby

As Cedric backed his fat, lazy arse down Silvia's driveway he had the cheek to ask her did she still want a coupon delivering next week. "Fuck off, you fat, lazy bastard before I roll the bloody coupon up into a tube shape and shove it up your fat, lazy arse."

Now reader, you may think this is a little harsh but let us not forget that this is the same man that Silvia lent her car to when his was out of action and again when his Father died and he didn't have transport for the funeral. This was the same man that had had his gutters repaired by Gorgeous because he was too fat and lazy to get his fat, lazy arse up a ladder to clear a bit of muck that was stuck in it and causing an overflow.

This was the same man that Silvia drove to with a spare set of keys when she had flu because the fat, lazy bastard had locked himself out of his car. But worst still this was the same man that on hearing that his wife had had a stroke in the middle of the night, came home from his night shift, made her a cup of tea and went back to work. She was paralysed down one side and couldn't get to the bathroom without dragging herself along the floor, using the banister and the radiators for support. He didn't even call the doctor.

This was the same man who left the household chores in the charge of their fourteen year old son, Damien and his much younger sister, Anita. It was lucky for Iris that Damien had wanted to be a chef and had practiced in her kitchen for years, baking cakes and roast dinners, or they would have starved. Cedric Shithead was totally useless. Iris had waited eleven years for him to knock the greenhouse down and longer still to replace a loose tile on the front door step.

When Silvia paid Iris a visit a few days later to check how she was doing, Cedric was wedged into a chair stuffing a trifle in his gob - courtesy of Damien - and watching television, totally oblivious to his surroundings and happy as a fat, lazy sand boy. Silvia looked upon him with disgust and wished it had been him who'd had the stroke. God forgave her.

"Why were people such bastards?" thought Silvia and felt a pang of guilt after posting her letter. She was fond of Iris, she'd helped Silvia with the ironing and was handsomely paid for it, she'd given Silvia fresh vegetables from their allotment, looked after her rabbits, "Bunny and Clyde" when she was on holiday and watered her plants. Her only doubt was that if Cedric Shithead lost his job then that would affect Iris's livelihood and Silvia couldn't stand that.

Luckily for everyone then that the letter was returned two weeks later - address unknown. Can you believe that? Posted in Liverpool, to the Liverpool address of the biggest company in Liverpool! Silvia could.

She disbanded the works syndicate and decided to switch pools companies to Zetters and do it on her own.

VIVA ESPAGNE

It was Belinda's birthday in April, and she always liked to plan a holiday for 'the gang' around that time. Every Boxing Day the ads would start on TV for all the sunny, exotic places you could go on holiday the following year. Belinda would scan the holiday brochures and find a cheap and cheerful deal in a hotel in sunnier climes.

This year she had her eye on a self-catering gaff in Benidorm and told the gang which hotel, how much and the dates they would be there. About a dozen booked but Silvia held back. She didn't fancy it at all and they were short of cash with the mortgage and bills to pay and decided she'd prefer to go away somewhere else later in the year, as April was always still a bit chilly, no matter where you were in Europe. It was that funny month between winter and spring and the weather didn't know quite what it was supposed to be doing, until one day the big switch was flicked and the sun came on full blast.

So when Silvia's birthday arrived in March, Gorgeous surprised her with a lovely card, a bouquet of flowers and a surprise note. She opened it and as she read it her faced dropped. "Oh no what have done?"

"I thought you'd want to go," he replied, hurt. "I know how much you love your holidays and I thought you wanted to be with your friends and only said no because of the money or lack of it, so I paid for the holiday so we can go."
"No, I said I didn't want to go because I am not keen on the place or the hotel, or the time of year as it will still be cool, and yes I am worried about the money because we don't have any and we still have to find money for spends and food, as none are included!" she said, exasperated.

There was no way to back out now, he'd paid and they'd lose the money if they cancelled. Silvia was so upset. On the drive to work all she could think about was the finances.
"How am I going to find the money for this now? As if things aren't bad enough," she fumed to herself.

During her lunch break she sat down with a pen and paper and wrote out all her expenses for the month. Council tax, gas, electric, water, insurance, food, phone bill, petrol, parking fees and any possibility of anything else popping up for payment she might have forgotten.
"I can probably scrimp and save about £20 a week and that would cover my holiday expenses," she said relieved.

When she arrived home, there was a stack of bills waiting to be opened along with a cheque from Zetters for £300.
"Oh my God!" she screamed.

"What's the matter?" asked Gorgeous.

"I've won the pools! I got 24 points! They sent a cheque for £300! We can afford the holiday now without having to worry about money at least!" she told him, relieved.

Silvia checked the newspaper for the results. If she'd stuck with Littlewoods they would have paid out £3000 that week as there were a lot more draws - ten times the amount, for 24 points. Any other week she might have won £1m for that and been able to retire and live off the interest, but as sod's law would have it, she was doomed to a life of frustratingly hard work, but at least for now her unwelcome present was being covered by the very welcome extra finances she'd won, to go to a place she disliked - even though she'd never been – and try and enjoy herself.

Fate – you are where you are meant to be. Fate wanted her to go.

ROBIN BASTARD

It was the same old story, the client couldn't make up his mind about the latest ad he was running, and consequently Silvia was into unpaid overtime again. The March nights were cold and at 7pm it was pitch black outside. The British Summer Time clock change would happen that weekend and she looked forward to lighter nights and the onset of spring.

To save her hard earned cash, Silvia had parked her car on a deserted car park on the edge of town, no longer privy to private, free car parking. After 7pm she knew no one ventured down there and now it was dark her car would be the only one left on the lot.

Silvia locked the office and walked in the direction of the car park. She had a strange sensation she was being watched and the hairs on the back of her neck stood on end. The wind blew a cellophane wrapper from a cigarette packet past her feet making a crinkling noise as it travelled along the pavement. She looked behind her but could only see the road disappearing round the corner and, of course, there was no one there.

She'd had the same feeling a few nights earlier. With both sides of the street being home to closed-down businesses she thought she'd heard the sound of someone stepping on a loose, metal grid cover. There was a loud bang which had made her jump, but as she peered into the darkness scanning the dead industrial estate, all she could see was the outline of a red picket fence and the blackness beyond.

Silvia had always been aware that it wasn't the safest place to park and carried her keys in her pocket to save fumbling in the dark depths of her handbag for them. Her sixth sense was buzzing. Something didn't feel right. She took the keys from her pocket and pulled out the blade of her Swiss Army knife, a present from Gorgeous (who was obsessed with gadgets) and meant as an implement to help out in emergencies like filing her nails - but tonight she had other ideas for its use, just in case, as she'd remembered her Mother's words about protecting herself, and the girls in her class filing their steel combs to a point to jab anyone who tried any funny business.

As she rounded the corner, a normally dormant pub was alive with revellers; Silvia smiled to herself and peered through the windows as she passed by thinking what a great time they were all having. It was the last Thursday of the month - pay day for most people and they were all enjoying spending it, too. She was tired and couldn't wait to get home.

She'd just celebrated another birthday and best of all it was Friday tomorrow, she could get out of stuffy suits and dress casual to work to help kick off the weekend. Then on Saturday she could go into town and spend the rest of the vouchers she'd been given as a birthday present. Her mind full of things to do she was distracted for a second when she inadvertently heard a noise behind her; she turned to see a man in dark clothing running towards her, his padded jacket making a rustling sound as the sleeves rubbed against the bodice as he moved ever closer. She knew what he wanted and stopped dead in her tracks.

"I've got a knife!" she screamed as he closed in on her and she lashed out with the implement in self-defence. She hacked away at his neck but his thick scarf and collar of his padded jacket were too much for the small blade to cope with. He said nothing. The bunch of keys rattled away as if they possessed some voodoo magic but it was no match for the "six foot twelve" monster who was wrestling her bag from her shoulders, snapping the strap with his bare hands.

 Silvia kept screaming and the monster never said a word. Once in his firm grasp he turned to run with his prize. In a split second all Silvia could think of was the treasured items in her bag; two silver coins engraved with "I Love You" from Gorgeous, her purse containing only 32p and the left over dregs of a favourite lipstick but more importantly a picture of her beautiful niece.

Then, the monster dropped her bag. Silvia caught her breath. She bent to retrieve it, but so did he. In a split second she toyed with the idea of kicking him in the head while he was bent over but stopped herself for fear she would be in more trouble if he got back up again.

She decided to let the Robin Bastard run off while she ran to her car still clutching the keys.

Adrenalin pumping, she raced across the wasteland of the car park, cutting herself on the extended blade as she fumbled for the car key. She jumped inside and locked the door. In a blind panic she searched for the small spanner that unlocked the steering lock, it was dark and she couldn't see properly. Her hand trembled with fright.
"Come on," she cried, "for God's sake!"

The adrenalin was pumping too fast, her heart racing a million miles an hour, her hand rotating faster than a Kenwood food mixer. She found it, fought with the lock and threw it to the floor, thrusting the key into the ignition she rammed the gears into reverse and bounced across the car park, quick hand break turn, thrust it into first and headed for the exit and Bootle Street Police Station.

Silvia parked up on double yellows - a fine was the least of her worries at this moment in time - and ran inside screaming, "Help, I've been mugged!"

Within minutes all her credit and bank cards had been cancelled, she'd been given a glass of water to calm her - but a brandy might have been better use - and now she had to call Gorgeous to tell him why she still hadn't arrived home.

Silvia started by informing him that she was OK.
"I'm OK," she said, "I'm in the police station and I've been mugged, but he didn't touch me, so don't panic."

Thirty minutes later he arrived at the police station with a big hug. It was another half hour before someone was free to take a statement.

Silvia had wiped the blood from her fingers and tried to bend the blade back into its cubbyhole but it wouldn't go. On closer inspection she noticed it was bent at a slight angle, she must have cut the monster's thick clothing - she wished it had been his neck, luckily for him his jugular was well protected. The monster even wore a knitted hat pulled down over his eyebrows so there was no guessing the colour of his hair. All Silvia had seen was a grey oval shape where his face should have been - she'd never be able to identify him except from the back and those bulky thighs as he ran off like a true athlete.

Silvia was in a quandary. Should she tell the police officer that she'd tried to defend herself with a blade, albeit a small one, or would she be in more trouble than her mugger? She decided to keep 'shtum'.

The PC informed her that this crime could not be classed as a mugging because he hadn't actually demanded that she give him her bag! So someone could walk up to you in the street and say "I say, old girl, do hand over your belongings so I can get my little dabs on your hard earned cash and go shoot up some drugs and have a fine old time at your expense!" Now that would be a mugging!

Silvia was furious, look at the state she was in, she was shaking like a leaf and that monster could get off scot free or at worst with handbag theft! Her attacker must have done this thing before. He must have known the rules. He must have planned it that way so if ever he got caught it would be on a minor charge. He was certainly more familiar with English Law than Silvia was. He was smart; she wished she'd cut his throat, left him to die, bleeding to death on the pavement outside the dodgy pub, she was so angry. The newspapers would report "A fight had broken out between rival drug gangs who frequented it and a young man was stabbed in the neck with a small, sharp instrument and died later in hospital from his injuries. Police are appealing for witnesses." Silvia wondered if she'd have been able to get away with it, just like he was doing now and there would be no witnesses from that pub.

She made her statement anyway; in case someone else had a similar incident then the net could close in on him. She hoped he was a drug addict and would overdose soon. Apparently bad breath was an indication of this, the PC informed Silvia, but it was undetectable through his scarf. She hoped he would come to a vicious end by a local drug baron, she hoped he would die painfully and slowly. She hoped he went cold turkey - the 32p he had stolen from her was hardly enough to get a fix of chips and gravy let alone a tablet of dodgy herbal substances.

She hoped he was bitterly disappointed with his ill gotten gains of a crushed lipstick, a facial spray at the end of its life, 32p, 2 now useless cards and a £20 gift voucher from Boots left over from her birthday, perhaps he could use it towards prescription methadone and take the lot in one go! She hoped he'd throw the broken bag into a skip and some kind person would find it and hand it in. But Silvia never saw or heard anything about it again.

That night Silvia couldn't sleep without seeing the monster run towards her in slow motion, grab the bag and run away again as she stood helpless, unable to move until the adrenalin kicked in.

It took Silvia a month before she could walk to the shops on her own again. All the time looking behind her, suspecting everyone in jeans and a bubble jacket was about to mug her again. In March that's 50% of the local population. By the time she made it back to the office after her first trip out she was in a lather of sweat but felt a great sense of achievement as she had jumped that huge hurdle and was back on the road to recovery.

Peeve instructed Silvia to order and issue all the women with personal alarms so they had some sort of defence if a similar thing were to happen to anyone else. Silvia changed car parks and even contemplated getting the train again in future. At least there would be plenty of other people around her if she did.

SPRING

The bags were packed with everything needed for a holiday abroad, beach towel, bikinis, shorts, t-shirts, and something a bit dressier for the evenings including a cardigan in case of chilly weather and hopefully the sun tan lotion she'd packed would get some use. They met the gang at the airport and after a quick drink boarded the flight for Spain and Benidorm.

Silvia was right about the weather, the first few days were cooler and her thick padded jacket she travelled in was still needed in the evenings, as it was pretty cold after dark.

At first they stayed local to their hotel, eating and drinking in the nearby bars and restaurants. Some of Belinda's friends had brought their young children along, so some of the others took turns to stay in with them so the parents could go out for a drink.

One night they decided to go out further afield and landed in a busy square with lots of bars and music playing. One bar was particularly packed and Silvia spied a pickpocket trying to unzip an unsuspecting female's shoulder bag.
"I don't like it here," she said to Gorgeous, "look at him trying to get into her bag."
Some of her group were at the bar trying to get a drink in the crush and one boy who was unsure of the currency held out his hand for the

barman to take what he needed. The other friends also tried to help at which the barman went crazy, "I honest, I honest!" he shouted.

"It's OK we're only trying to help," they explained.

He was having none of it, and Silvia started to feel more uncomfortable.

"I don't feel safe here," she told Belinda, " I've seen a pickpocket and now this, we're going to finish our drinks and go back."

"Ok, what a shame, I'll see you tomorrow then," replied her friend.

That night Silvia was woken, in the early hours of the morning by the slamming of a door. "It must be the parents coming back from the night out," she thought and went back to sleep.

Next morning they got up and went for breakfast before going to the pool to meet up with the others. They all seemed very quiet and she thought they must be hungover. She looked at one of them and saw he had a black eye.

"What happened to you?" she asked, as she noticed he also had stitches in his eyebrow.

"You know that bar we were in?" he proceeded to tell her, "well after you left a guy tried to pickpocket me, I felt him take the wallet from my shirt pocket so I grabbed him to try and get it back, but he must have had accomplices as we think it was passed back through the crowd. Then the barman called the police and threw us out, but there was a crowd of Spaniards outside with bottles waiting for us. They smashed one of them over my head and into my face, fortunately it caught my eyebrow," he said turning to show her the back of his head, also sporting stiches.

"Jesus," Silvia said, horrified, "I am so glad we left."

"Yes, we had to go to hospital for treatment then the police station to report it.

There was a list of incidents on the desk and it was full of things like robbed, mugged, beaten, over and over again," he told her.

Silvia was scared; she felt like crying and looked over at Gorgeous, as if to confirm that this is why she never wanted to come to Benidorm.

"I promise I will never, ever book anywhere, ever again when you say you don't want to go," he said forlornly.

"I just feel so scared now, I have never, ever felt scared on a holiday before. We've only been here four days and still have another 10 to go in this hell hole," she whimpered.

"It's OK," said Belinda, "we'll steer clear of the centre from now on and just stay local in the English bars."

Silvia counted every day like it was a prison sentence, till it was time to go home, and vowed she would never, ever go back.

WITH FRIENDS LIKE THESE

Silvia was having twinges again and knew it was time for another dreaded trip to the dentist. Not for her a simple check up and "No fillings this time! Thank you very much, see you in six months." No, every time she went it was a major co-ordination between dentist, hygienist and technician to fill, scrape, polish and rebuild her mouth using the latest technologies.

She envied Americans with those huge, white smiles and teeth that can do some damage to a club sandwich. Why, they even look like they have twice as many teeth as the British - so why couldn't Silvia have some of theirs?

Even when she was little and saw the school dentist - the whole class had to form a line, while one by one they filed in to take their place in his makeshift surgery - she'd been afraid of the ghoul-like figure in his bleached white coat wearing bottle-end spectacles.

"Too many sweets!" he'd boom, "these need to come out, make an appointment." He was probably thrown out of the Gestapo for cruelty.

Sitting in his waiting room on her return, Silvia had to endure rows upon rows of small children, some of them her friends, being dragged screaming and kicking into his surgery by their distraught parents and being carried out again all limp and semi-conscious with the after effects of the gas.

Silvia was in a state of shock by the time her Mother helped her into the 'Big Black Chair'. The bright lights of the overhead dazzled her eyes, and then the gas mask was placed over her nose and mouth threatening to suffocate her, the smell of the gas churning her stomach. Her hand fell limp from her Mother's grasp. She was alone with the Devil and his instruments of torture.

With her Mother ushered out of the room the nightmare began. Under the influence of the gas Silvia was transformed into a little pink bubble car with windows of wide, frightened eyes looking around in the darkness at something chasing her, speeding faster and faster. The more she tried to get away the more it seemed she couldn't escape. The eyes looking back at something scary and unknown while her suspension rhythmically bobbed her up and down in her panic to flee and shouting "no, no, get off me you bastard!" as the gas wore off.

Suddenly she was awake and could see her horrified Mother apologising profusely to the dentist that she had no idea how Silvia, a mere six year old, came to know such language. Silvia's Mother dragged her out of the 'Big Black Chair', still dopey from the anaesthetic, and bid him good day.

Once outside Silvia's Mother exclaimed, "I've never been so embarrassed in all my life!" and would never take her back to that dentist ever again!

And so she didn't. For it was many years that passed before Silvia visited that great institution "Let's Whip Them All Out" Dental Surgery again, and then only in cases of extreme emergencies or pain, which was at about the age of eight.

Silvia had been enjoying a game in the school playground, which involved running from one end to the other. She was a good and fast runner and beat most of the other kids. Until she tripped, (or so she thought) fell and smashed one of her teeth in half, her newly, just grown by an eight year old, never to be repeated offer, second teeth. The pain was unbelievable, followed by a strong throbbing when the feeling slowly found its way back into the tooth. Then the sting of the cold air, on the exposed nerve.

At that very moment, Silvia's Mother sensed something was wrong and looked at a picture of her daughter she had in the house. She couldn't fathom out the strange feeling she had all afternoon, her sixth sense felt like it had been wired in to the electricity. Then Silvia returned home.

A new dentist said he could fix it but when Silvia asked if it would hurt, he was too honest, he should have lied. Silvia didn't go back until the tooth was so painful and rotted that it had to come out.

For years afterwards Silvia only smiled with her lips clamped tightly shut and it became an automatic reaction to cover her mouth with her hand when she laughed. She wished she had broken her nose instead. At least they would have straightened it out a little when they reset it.

It was years later when recalling the story to her old school friends that Silvia discovered that someone had in fact tripped her up, jealous of her popularity and speed. Fate – you are where you are meant to be.

***

It had been a great summer evening in the local park, a game of bat and ball on the tennis court and muck about on the putting green. It was so warm that the Park Ranger thought it might just thunder. Silvia hated storms; she hated the lightening, which always made her jump, and the loudness of the thunder always scared her.

She was warm from the games and went to the water fountain for a drink. A queue formed behind her. As she lowered her head over the metal spout to take a mouthful of cool water there was a jostle from the back, then suddenly the numbness, the throbbing, the sting of the cold water as a piece of her front tooth circumnavigated the bowl and flushed itself down the drain like the ball in a roulette wheel rolling round and dropping into 17 Black.

Someone had pushed her head down onto it, smashing her other front tooth in half. Silvia ran home crying, not even stopping to find out who the culprit was. Some kids break bones. Silvia broke teeth. It took another four years before she plucked up the courage to go to the dentist again.

Silvia's Mother had heard good reports about new dentist in the area and as Silvia was approaching puberty, it wouldn't be long before she gained an interest in boys, she thought. But boys could be cruel the older they got and somehow she had to try to persuade her daughter that something had to be done before it was too late. She put the suggestion into Silvia's head and never said another word. Two days later Silvia crept into her Mother's bedroom on her way out to school and asked her mum to make her an appointment. Reverse psychology, works every time.

The appointment was duly made and Silvia's Mother instructed her on what to say to the dentist. Silvia memorized this in-between trying to stop her knees knocking together with fear, sounding like a pair of castanets. She could have joined the percussion section of the school orchestra, the noise they were making.

Mr. Lovely Dentist was very nice. He suggested some remedies but Silvia was blind to them and could only repeat the ones that her Mother had trained her to say, to take them out and have false ones.

Silvia's Mother said, "You can have the needle in the arm this time, I'm not having you embarrass me again like last time, you know you swear with gas!"
He was reluctant and tried to change her mind, the teeth around the gap were healthy and would only need filling and a small bridge. Silvia agreed to this lesser torture.

He began to drill - for oil in Texas, Silvia guessed, he was at it that long. The more appointments she went to, the more relaxed she became until the knocking knees subsided and then eventually stopped. Silvia's confidence slowly returned. The major foundation work done, it was time to build the Menai Bridge.

Treatment over, Silvia recited the alphabet to make sure there was no whistle when she spoke but happy that at last she had a smile she could be proud of again and kept regular appointments until Mr. Lovely Dentist emigrated to Australia.

Every six months there was a different dentist. They all wanted to drill out her old fillings and replace them. That's when she got the infection.

At first she thought it was just sore gums, but the mouthwash dentist No. 5 gave her didn't help. Then they started to bleed so dentist No. 6 said brush harder to strengthen the gums. Then they started to wobble like piano keys and dentist No. 7 took an X-ray, informed her of the bone loss and said that they would have to come out.

Silvia was horrified that they'd all let it get this bad through their neglect. If they'd taken X-rays in the beginning they might have saved her teeth. She went to the dental hospital for a second opinion only to have it confirmed by dentist No. 8. She left; complete with teeth so pliable that Beethoven could have composed a symphony on them.

A friend told her of a cosmetic dentist whose method was prevention rather than cure. She herself was thinking of going to get two millimetres drilled off her gleaming, white, wonderful front teeth because she thought they were a tad too long.
Silvia was mortified, "Why on earth would you want to do that to yourself? I'd swop with you anyway."
"Each to her own," she replied, "It would give my confidence a boost!"

Like she needed it, Lilly was the most confident person Silvia knew. Men had been known to pass out at her feet, dazzled by her beautiful green eyes and tousled blonde highlighted hair. Once, one of them pushed his hand into Silvia's face to push her out of the way so he could get a better look a Lilly.

Silvia made an appointment with dentist No. 9, Lilly didn't. He confirmed the wobbly teeth would need to come out, but at least this dentist wasn't about to leave the country or palm her off with a locum every six months. She kept regular appointments, again. Silvia was now happy and her own confidence returned.

Silvia was mad; Gorgeous had never been to the dentist for years and only needed a filling! Every time Silvia went it was a major refit! It wasn't fair. It seemed she was having his fillings as well as her own.

She got an abscess. She couldn't understand it. She'd brushed, flossed, gargled with antiseptic mouthwash and still she got infections.

But this was no ordinary abscess. It refused to be drained by a root canal and called for an apicoectomy - the most horrific thing Silvia had experienced in her life. And an introduction to dentist no. 10.

Cut from nose to ear along the gum - after millions of injections to numb the area - she was operated on in the jawbone with a machine that sounded like a pneumatic drill, rattling the brain and grinding away at the bone to remove the infection. The abscess was reluctant to let go; it clung to the tooth root like a leech. She prayed it would be over soon whilst gripping the arms of the chair.

Then he was in her sinus, which filled with blood. Silvia thought she would drown. She couldn't breath through her nose and her mouth was full of instruments. "Swallow," he shouted, "you'll be ok." Silvia obeyed and thought at this rate she could give Linda Lovelace a run for her money.

Swabbed out, the gum was sealed with a piece of grandma's thick, black, knitting yarn in a lovely blanket stitch.
"You can go back to your own dentist in a week to have them removed," he announced.
"Gee, thanks." cringed Silvia. "Remind me never to ask you to knit me a scarf!"

An hour later the anaesthetic began to wear off. The agony, the pain, the stinging like a paper cut on the gums. The soluble aspirin did the trick, working its magic within seconds of being passed over the wound and a hot water bottle nursed against the cheek helped stun the pain and Silvia began to relax. Before the week was over the wound was healed and Silvia began to spit the stitches out one by one. By the time she got back to the dentist a week later there was nothing left for him remove.

Never again thought Silvia, but eighteen months later she awoke one morning with a dull throbbing in the side of her cheek and realised that there it was again that familiar feeling of dread that another abscess was on the way, and the whole process was repeated with dentist no 11. The scalpel, the Black and Decker drill, the water drowning her. She prayed the next week would pass quickly and that the pain would decrease a little each day.

Back at no.9 Silvia asked about an alternative to the plate. No. 9 said he could fit a bridge, Silvia christened it the Humber and so her lower teeth gleamed like new again, never to be removed, a permanent fixture.
Silvia thought how the pain must be like having a baby, a few months later and you forget how awful it really was and try for another.

After an hour with the Black and Decker and mounds of glue and putty like substances being thrust into her mouth on U-shaped palettes, she was all set. Fitted with temporary crowns and told to come back next week for the final fitting.
"Oh, and by the way," he said, "don't eat any curry or these will turn yellow!"
"Great, corporal punishment and my favourite food banned for a week. Even prisoners on death row get their last meal," she thought.

Four hours later, Silvia began to worry why the anaesthetic hadn't begun to wear off. It usually only takes an hour but this guy really pumped her full of the stuff. Gorgeous thought she'd had a stroke! She slobbered her hot Earl Grey tea down her front and constantly bit her tongue although she couldn't feel either.

A week later Silvia was back in the chair being injected with more green liquid like filling the car from the unleaded pump. The temporaries were tugged free and the fitting of her new smile began. She christened this one the Runcorn.

"Not long now," thought Silvia, mouth full of instruments.

"How do they look?" asked the dentist.

"Great!" Silvia exclaimed, admiring his handy work. She had her beautiful smile back again.

"Just a few adjustments, and we'll cement them in."

That's when the trouble started but Silvia wouldn't know it until she got the feeling back in her mouth. She left the surgery feeling full of confidence - gleaming teeth smiling forth.

Silvia awoke the next morning with toothache. The dentist said it was just tenderness and would settle in a few days. Then there was the unusual whistle she'd developed because of the air passing through the different gaps in her teeth. She sounded like a lisping Sir Lancelot from the cartoon of King Arthur; every time she pronounced the letter 's' a great whistle of air would flow from her mouth. 'Yessss, ssssire, at your sssservicccccce.'

Silvia did her best to avoid words with 's' in them for fear of dogs barking and Irish marching bands forming a queue behind her, but to no avail.

A few days passed and Silvia was still in pain, she went back to the dentist. He assured her all was well, removed a few huge scrapings of cement he'd overlooked from under her gums and sent her packing. "That should do it," he said. It didn't.

The pain was incredible, and she suffered for days. Then a colleague recommended his dentist No.12. She worked a miracle. She discovered that three of Silvia's teeth had become live and had to remove the nerve of one of them. She plugged them with temporary fillings but refused to touch the bridge saying Silvia would have to go back to her own dentist for him to sort it.

Silvia did. Early the next morning she turned up at the surgery of No. 9 before it opened demanding something was done. The dentist was more interested in taking a phone call from his mistress and ignored Silvia lying in pain in the big black chair.

"Bloody charming," Silvia thought, "what a complete bastard. It must be his mistress, he wouldn't talk to his wife at 8.30am after just leaving the house and now he's mentioning my name to the caller so it had to be a nurse at the surgery who'd been in on the operation. Who else would know who she was?"

Silvia felt a joke was being made at her expense; she was furious, angry and upset. She knew exactly who it was. His assistant - bubbly, laughed too much at his jokes, worshipped the ground he practiced on and probably shagged him in the very chair Silvia was now lying on! Oh, yes, he was definitely sowing more than gums.

After a fruitless session, Silvia returned a few days later with Gorgeous in tow. He finally took notice and checked her bite (which should have been the first thing he did after fitting the bridge) realised his mistake and adjusted it with more drilling, apologised for her feeling fobbed off and told her to call anytime.

Fobbed off and pissed off was exactly how Silvia felt, that he'd only actually done something when she'd brought the heavies with her and he'd completely ignored her pleas for help when she'd phoned the emergency number on a Sunday only to be told by him that he was entitled to a day off!
"Then why give out an emergency number to call, you dick head?" Silvia thought to herself. "What a complete prick."

The next day Silvia's pain had eased by 50%. Thank God, she was all set to call her solicitor and sue but as she still had three temporary fillings to fix she reconsidered and gave him a second chance. All fixed and paid up the sum of £350 Silvia was pain free for six months. Then the twinges started again.

Silvia couldn't understand it. It was the tooth with the root canal that No. 12 had taken the live nerve out of. She's had root canals before and never had any trouble after them. No nerve, no pain. But there was definitely something suspect going on. Every morning when she woke it was painful but would ease off during the first hour or so.

Silvia made an appointment with dentist No.12 again, reluctant to go back to dentist (I can't keep my dick in my pants) No. 9. She X-rayed and discovered that the root canal that he should have done six months earlier, hadn't been done and had left the root canal empty and just filled the tooth! The gum had become infected and needed cleaning out. She set to work. She cauterised the infection, filled the canal and finished off the tooth with a temporary filling again to see if it calmed down.

Silvia enquired about white fillings. She'd heard that they were healthier and would certainly help her smile to look more bright and as she needed two more fillings anyway it made sense to do them white. No. 12 obliged. But after the anaesthetic wore off Silvia was in great pain again. She had not mentioned to Silvia that white fillings are much harder and can cause their own problems. The bite was too high and caused the nerve in the tooth to react.

"Oh, the pain," moaned Silvia. Every time she bit together a sharp pain shot up into her head, her ear, four teeth on the top and two on the bottom would ache and the gland under her jaw would throb. Silvia returned on several occasions to have a little bit here drilled off and a little bit there drilled off, but after two weeks of backwards and forwards to the chair (and it was now October) there was no give in the pain. Even after constant reassuring that there would be. And she had this strange sensation where her right jawbones met, near her ear.

Silvia was beside herself. Here she was a month after her first visit still in pain but from a different source, and she'd paid another £120 for the privilege. The dentist fobbed her off with antibiotics and said she must have an infection although nothing showed on the X-ray. She returned again and the receptionist shouted at her, "Silvia! You have to give the antibiotics a chance to work."

"But what do I do in the meantime? I'm in dreadful pain, I can't eat anything, it's making me sick and I'm losing weight at a rate of knots!" Silvia cried and stormed out of the surgery. She never went back.

Throughout this hideous ordeal, Silvia was also trying to hold down her busy job. The amount of time spent in the dentist chair was heightening her stress levels. She needed to stop travelling great distances on other's recommendations to find the perfect dentist, she needed to be nearer home to make it easier to get to work.

Silvia went back to the trouser snake to see if he could help but he was neither use nor ornament. He drilled out the new filling and put a temporary in to see if it would calm down. 24 hours later the pain was back. Silvia went back to him 2 days later.

"I'm still having trouble", she told him. "It's this strange sensation in my jaw, every time it goes off I'm sick."

"Give it time, it will settle," he said reassuringly.

Two days later Silvia was back in the surgery. "I'm still having trouble, it hasn't calmed down," she said.

"Give it time," he said, again.

Two days later Silvia returned. "It's still not right," she said, "can you do a root canal?"

"Not on a molar," he laughed in her face. "You'll have to have it out!"

She wanted to punch him in the nose. Here she was in terrible pain, yet again and he was totally unsympathetic, and quite willing to leave her in a state of stress. What a rotten bedside manner!

In desperation Silvia consulted a private specialist. The first thing he suggested was to try a rubber-like temporary filling to cushion the tooth when chewing and hopefully calm the nerve. If that didn't work, he would do a root canal!
"On a molar?" asked Silvia.
"Of course," he answered, and was surprised when Silvia told him of her previous conversation with dick for brains.

At last something was beginning to work, she could see the light at the end of the tunnel (it was now November). She'd lost 7lbs in weight and her trousers resembled a Bedouin tent, billowing in the wind as she walked.

A week later, the tooth was refilled but it didn't cure that strange sensation in her jawbone. Then the oddest thing happened, the tooth dick head had forgotten to root canal was becoming active again, like a festering volcano waiting to erupt into a septic flow of puss from an abscess and it made her vomit again.

Silvia was in such a state that she couldn't eat her Sunday lunch when the family went out to celebrate her Father's 65th Birthday. Everyone was tucking into superb roasts with all the trimmings and all Silvia could manage was a mouthful of Salmon, which met her stomach coming up on the way down. It was the 23rd November.

Silvia was beginning to feel weak; she'd hardly eaten a thing in two months. Her taste buds had changed and food she once loved to eat were no longer palatable. She was limited to things her stomach would allow to pass through like egg mayonnaise sandwiches, omelettes, mash potatoes and soup.

Silvia's boss had booked a special Christmas office party - an overnight stay in Paris! Silvia was not looking forward to going in the state she was in. She decided she'd go home and pack her overnight bag, get an early night and hoped she would feel much better by the time early morning came for the 6am flight to Paris. It was the 12th December.

Silvia rang the dentist again and explained her symptoms. "I've been sick as a parrot, my other tooth is hurting now and I have this pain in my jaw that makes my stomach churn. It tightens my throat so I can't swallow anything, and every time I put food to my mouth my stomach comes up to meet it and I missed my trip to Paris! I couldn't possibly go like this and let everyone else feel miserable too."

An X-ray revealed that the root canal, hadn't been done deep enough and he would have to redo it. That's when they discovered a lateral crack and there was no option but to take it out.
"Can you do it now?" Silvia asked. "This has gone on long enough and it's Christmas in 3 days, I don't want to be ill over Christmas!"

And so the tooth came out and with it a load of infection. He scraped away at the gaping hole it left to clear out the puss and sent her packing with homeopathic Arnica for heeling, Colloidal silver for infections, and Dentox for bruising during trauma. Silvia was also on her second lot of antibiotics and painkillers - she should have bought shares in Boots the amount of Ibuprofen she'd taken in the last three months. But at least now the pain should start to ease off and get a little better each day. "I'll be right as rain by Christmas Day," she thought. "Just in time to enjoy a traditional family dinner. Hey, what's that I can smell? It's bullshit!"

On Christmas Eve Silvia paid a visit to the doctor to explain the sickness. He prescribed Motilium (they give this to cancer patients on chemotherapy to stop the nausea) but they didn't work, no sooner had she swallowed them than her head was over the sink bringing them back up again. She was a human geyser.

By Christmas Day Silvia was still in agony and finding it difficult to keep anything down. She forced in some omelette in the hope that the protein might give her strength to see her through the day and she couldn't take the painkillers on an empty stomach especially with a concoction of homeopathic remedies. She was now ten pounds lighter and felt like a walking Molotov cocktail.

Dosed up to the eyeballs, she put on her brave face and ventured out to face the in-laws and the out-laws, present swapping, trying to be happy for their sake so as not to ruin their day. The only saving grace was her brother-in-law who just happened to be suffering from the same thing, so they passed most of the time by exchanging stories and tablets.

Boxing Day was a big get-together with friends Silvia hadn't seen for months. A tour of the local pubs in the City Centre she also hadn't seen for months. It was lucky that all the clothes she'd bought for the party season the previous year were still in good shape for this one. She hadn't seen the inside of a clothes shop in so long, which was just as well as the money she'd saved on clothes and food had now been spent at the dentist. So far she was into about another £180 - £90 for the root canal and then another £90 for the privilege of extracting the same tooth, bloody cheek! Plus the 120 quid it cost for the new white filling in the spasming tooth that also showed no sign of improvement.

The evening didn't go too well. She couldn't drink much for starters, afraid that the mixture of pills and remedies may prove fatal with alcohol! The only one sober amongst her tipsy pals, Silvia felt miserable. It was only when one of the couples starting airing their dirty washing in public that Silvia cut her losses and returned home to fester in private.

Over the next few days friends came to visit the wet lettuce called Silvia, lain out on the couch in a now baggy jogging suit. She must be the only person alive who didn't put on weight over Christmas! And then on the morning of the 30th she awoke and the pain had gone. From a scale of 1-10 it had been 10 the previous evening when she'd gone to bed and now it was zero. Silvia counted that she'd been retching for 9 consecutive days and was now 12lbs lighter.

Silvia hadn't missed a party on New Year's Eve ever since she was old enough to attend them. Whether it was at her Mother's house as a teenager, down the local disco with the Adonis of the day or a meal out with friends and then back to someone's house for a party, Silvia always made sure she saw the Old Year out and the New Year in, in style. Even that time going to Mexico, choosing a good Christian country that would still celebrate and make it even more special.

But not this year. Silvia divided her time between chucking her guts up, watching old movie repeats on the telly and sleeping off the shaking fits. At midnight she went outside to listen to the foghorns sounding and watch the fireworks people had saved from Bonfire night. The neighbours asked her in for a drink. Not one to go to a party empty handed, Silvia retrieved a dusty bottle of champagne from the back of a kitchen cupboard. Wiping it down she thought to herself, "Well, if nothing else, it may kill off some bacteria and help me sleep!"

She ventured forth and explained her predicament and begged a pardon for looking so scruffy on such a prestigious occasion, only to discover that two other party members had had the same trouble with dentist no. 9. To one he'd wanted to crown perfectly healthy teeth just because they had a stain on them, which later came off when he polished them after a regular visit.

The other had had a bridge fitted, which lasted only three years and fell out. She was then told that the teeth were damaged and would have to be removed and a plate fitted. The poor woman was devastated. She'd always looked after her teeth with pride and here she was embarrassed to even talk about it. Silvia was mad. Mad because the git was advising people to have unnecessary treatment and they trusted him.

Whether it was the champagne or whether it was the stories from the previous night that made Silvia feel like she wasn't alone in her suffering but she made a miraculous improvement - which was just as well as it was her Mother's birthday and she'd managed to plan a few surprises, a few meals out and even shopped for presents! The sickness stayed away for thirteen days - unlucky for some – but her Mother's lucky number!

I BOUGHT MY BOSS A PORSCHE

Silvia always bought cards for people, for their birthdays, their engagements, their weddings and their funerals. On her birthday she always took cakes into work for everyone, her Boss stuffed one in his gob and didn't even wish her a happy birthday - TWAT - even though he passed her three times that day. He was still in accusational mode over a job that had gone terribly wrong and blamed Silvia as he'd lost a lot of money. But it wasn't Silvia's fault. She'd been trying to deal with a petulant creative who threw his rattle out of his pram if he didn't get his own way and an account executive who couldn't make a decision. Then there was a botched booking in a Nice hotel for the Christmas Party, which the accountant had made and inadvertently got the date wrong when he asked his travel agent to book them all into a hotel the week before they were supposed to go. Silvia had only booked the flights - for the correct day.

Silvia arrived into work the week before the departure and received a
phone call from the Travel Agent. "Where were you?"
"What do you mean? We are going this weekend," she explained.
"No you booked in last weekend. There is a conference on this
weekend and there is no availability now for hotels."
"How did that happen, I booked the flights myself for the correct date?"
"The accountant said last weekend. I faxed over the confirmations."

Silvia had a look at them, but they were illegible. It was impossible to
tell what date they were as the ink was so faint on the originals he'd
faxed over that the machine couldn't duplicate what wasn't there. She
had to tell her Boss what happened. His blood pressure rose to 300
over 190, and his face went the colour of borscht soup, but he blamed
Silvia. Silvia rebooked all the hotel rooms herself in the only apparent
hotel available in the whole of Nice – a 2 star Comfort Inn but she
wasn't happy and penned a letter.

Dear Boss,

For 10 years I have helped you build your empire. I have cut your
expenditure, I have controlled your budgets, and I have made you
richer by increasing your cash flow. I have been who you wanted me
to be but not been myself. I have dressed how you preferred and felt
restricted in my movements, I need to go back to me, the original me,
the happy me. My focus has been blurred by a fog called overwork
and stress. No one is my friend and I am a friend to no one. My life is
not my own, how I would like to live it.

I want to wake up in the morning and smile, not wish to turn back over
and fall back asleep and pray I didn't have to get up and drag my arse
into the shower or worry whether my hair would dry quickly enough. Is
there enough time for breakfast? What should I wear today? Will the
motorway be clear, will there still be a space in the car park by the
time I get in? Can I walk faster to work to save a minute or two? Will

that bloody red light on the phone be flashing – someone demanding my attention before I've even got my coat off! Mouth dry but no time to get a cup of tea yet or go to the loo.

Deadlines to meet, everyone moaning about everyone else. Trying to stay calm and not having to explain my actions and myself when I shouldn't have to. I pull everyone out of the shit not just myself. I have a right to have some joy in my life. I obsess about foreign places because I don't want to be here. I want a life where I feel I am on holiday everyday. I don't like this person you have created – and neither do you. I frighten you and I frighten myself.

Like Frankenstein, it's time to unplug the monster to reveal the real, happy person trapped inside the multiple body parts and personalities. I want my life back. I want to dance and sing at the top of my voice, to laugh, to touch, to smell, to feel, to hear, to taste life and I want it to be a gastronomical feast. I have a wardrobe where I hang all my disguises for work. They are all dull colours. Winter. Then there is my life wardrobe. It's full of pastel shades of pinks, blues, greens, lilacs and summer.

I don't want an obituary that says here lies Silvia Fernsby who died of complications of living someone else's idea of life and doing ten years of crap and not doing what she really wanted to do, attempting to fill the boredom with cars, houses, jewellery, food and worrying whether she should get her ears pierced, finally she succumbed 20 years too early. She was found dead at her desk and it took colleagues 2 days to notice because they'd never really asked her how she felt.

I have been totally unselfish to your needs at the expense of my own. I abandoned the things that were important to me so you wouldn't be disappointed. I have never felt happy since I left Liverpool, I am not welcome here but have tried to ignore it – I hate Manchester, it's grim, the weather, the town and the majority of people who work here don't live here but it was me who looked forward to working here for a change of scene.

There's been a lot of bitching in the office lately, mainly about one person who you won't have a bad word said against because you think the sun shines out of her arse, but it hasn't come from me although you think it has, why?

And now you're making excuses to me for the new car you've bought her saying she only got an upgrade because her sugar daddy paid the extra into the kitty, oh, and by the way he just happens to be a client and a golfing partner, and she needs a little something to enhance her life and pose to the neighbours with. I don't care about what anyone else gets but what have you given me to enhance my life?

No wonder your accounts lady embezzled you. She probably had the right idea. If it isn't forthcoming - take it anyway. She saw more than I did, the cars, the salaries, the expense accounts, the fat bonus payments and she saw all the people who did all the work to pay for those things get sweet fanny adams in return, so I guess she thought she'd take a slice of the cake, too - but forget to ask first!

As for me, I couldn't give a monkeys what car you drive, how big your house is or what time the Securicor van is delivering your wages, if I can't hold a decent conversation with you and get intelligent answers then you're off my Christmas list.

And just because I don't speak with a posh accent and wear designer clothes doesn't mean I have no ambition. And just because my ambitions aren't the same as yours - to play for Man U - doesn't mean that they are worthless. So stop making me feel like the poor relation who has to be pitied because half of our clients speak like I do and they don't all want a stuck up cow dealing with them.

When you first started in business, the same person I am now helped you grow, nurtured your very few clients, and made you the profitable company you are today. You knew my working for you would influence people and nothing has changed.

I have smiled at your clients, I've been called a liar by many of them and had to grin and bear it when really I felt like giving them a piece of my mind and telling them to piss off! That's why I have to write to you now because you never stand still long enough to listen to what I have to say. If I crack a joke everyone will laugh except you - all you say is don't give up your day job.

I feel there is no place for me here anymore. My decisions don't seem to count and you're certainly not interested in my opinions although I am right 90% of the time. I can't do anything without people wanting to know what I am doing and checking everything I do.

How come the others can swan off to see clients (with a little shopping thrown in for good measure), turn up at the last hour and demand that the jobs they forgot to brief me on should be done first over everyone else's?

Hey, but who said life was fair? If you've got the right accent and a designer wardrobe then you're laughing and if hubby's a client well, let's throw in a sports car, too.

But while you're mucking about on the golf course, spare a thought for those job bags on my desk, not going anywhere fast and looming deadlines, impossible to meet - but I meet them. And me, tearing my hair out in sheer frustration, demented because I can't get anyone to listen to me let alone give me five minutes at the beginning of a job to save half a day of amends at the end of it. Hey, I'm all right Jack - thanks for asking - but Silvia may need a little help and understanding from time to time!

Since I've been working for you I've had nothing but bad luck, I've crashed my car, had to give up college because I can't get away early enough to take the bloody lessons, scalded my hand, been mugged, had tooth ache for 18 months, had teeth extracted, had dental operations complete with a gob full of stitches and suffered terrible infections that made me miss a trip to Paris that I'd paid for, too, lose twelve pounds in weight through vomiting uncontrollably most mornings over an eight-month period and nearly lost my brother to Cancer, and actually lost my Grandmother to Cancer - and I've still managed to get to work. What other member of staff has given you the same backup?

Yours faithfully,
Silvia.

Silvia wrote it all down to get it off her chest but never ever sent it. "Maybe I'll write a book and he can read about it in there," she thought. "At least I'll make a few bob from it and maybe buy my own sports car as well."

The weekend in Nice went well, and after a lovely evening meal and a trip on the train to Monte Carlo casino, they all indulged in a little gambling. Silvia could never fathom the roulette tables; although her sixth sense used to kick in now and again, she was afraid to put money down on the table. She remembered a similar night out in Tenerife, where she stood staring at the numbers and thought James Bond always bets on 17 black and it came in and the number 6 popped into her head (her Mother's birthday) it came up, but she hadn't bet anything. She might have walked out of there with a fist full of pesetas that would have paid for the trip.

Some of the team left to have a drink in a little place down the road, but Silvia stayed with three girls and the accountant to try her hand.

While Silvia was on the poker machines, after a quick lesson from him on how to play, the other girls were being chatted up by a garishly dressed Italian, in mustard trousers with a Ferrari parked outside (probably in a matching colour). He invited them to a party back in Italy just over the border. Fortunately they had the sense to say no and promptly linked arms with the accountant who led them to safety away from him. The look on his face said it all, "What's he got that I haven't?"

"Not mustard coloured kex that's for sure!" laughed Silvia.

They all met back at the Café de Paris to make the return journey to Nice on the train and again the group divided into two when they arrived. Some who could keep their eyes open went onto a club and the few that couldn't went back to the hotel. Silvia went back to the hotel. She was lucky enough to have had a room to herself but the next morning at breakfast she discovered that when the accountant had got back to the hotel he didn't have a key for his room as he was sharing with the boss and he was still out playing. So he spent the night on the sofa in reception and was so soundly asleep that he didn't hear the boss returning to the comfort of his room in the early hours.

Karma. What goes around comes around. Turned out Nice again after all.

MOVING HOUSE

Silvia thought it would be easy. She'd seen a nice area nearer to work, easy motorway access, decent sized houses now all she needed was to find one and sell theirs.

One Saturday morning they bought the local newspaper and went to the local pub to scour the pages to see what was on offer, get a few numbers and called a few estate agents to make appointments.

As they walked into the pub, all the customers stopped what they were doing and turned to look at Silvia and Gorgeous as though they had just landed from outer space.
"Weirdos," Silvia whispered to Gorgeous.

There were only 4 houses available for sale in the area they wanted. "This house buying lark is dead easy!" she exclaimed. "I don't know what all the fuss is about. Why all the stress?"

Their first viewing was a detached 3-bed that was being rented by the sister of a man who worked abroad. They had a dog locked out in the back garden, which refused to stop barking, so they couldn't go out to view that part. On seeing the upstairs bathroom with the inner cardboard roll of a toilet roll stuffed down the loo, they looked at each other and decided they'd seen enough.

Second was another 3-bed. The husband showed them round the house while the wife and mother sat smoking on the sofa, totally uninterested. Then
another, where the couple had left their teenage son to show them around. On walking up the stairs the smell of sweaty socks got stronger and stronger and when they went into the bathroom and saw they hadn't even bothered to flush the toilet they left in disgust.

The final house they went to look at was a 3-bed detached with a spa bath. The bedrooms were smaller and you'd be prone to banging your head on the wall when you got out of bed. Downstairs was much larger with open plan kitchen/diner and a conservatory. The kitchen cabinets had glass doors, so she could finally show off all her Kutani fine bone china that her Father had brought back from Japan after the war, and she'd inherited after her Grandmother had passed away, nobody wanting it and so she rescued it from going in the bin.

It was nicely decorated, so they'd only need to plonk their furniture on the carpets and the setting would be perfect. They put in an offer and put their own house up for sale. After 6 months and only 3 people coming to view, one being a doctor with 6 bikes and asthma who brought his parent along from Sheffield and declared it too small.

They changed estate agents and remarketed their house but it took another 6 months before an older couple looking to downsize fell in love with it and put in an offer. It all rested on a guy they couldn't trace who was at the end of the chain and the only phone number they had was his elderly mother's!

Silvia and Gorgeous were about to go on holiday for the Millennium, so informed their buyer not to worry, as nothing would probably happen over the holiday period between Christmas and New Year. When they arrived back home there was a telephone message waiting for them. It was their buyers, saying the chain had sold and they panicked because they couldn't get in touch and had found another house. Nothing from the estate agent, but the elusive bloke at the end of the chain had suddenly appeared the day after they left and they whole chain sold – without them.

They lost the house again and so their search began again.
Only 4 houses were for sale, all 4-bed this time with ensuites and conservatories and bigger bedrooms. They chose one and their offer was accepted now they just had to wait for a buyer.

Next followed months of offers being rejected because first time buyers couldn't get their mortgage offers due to bad debts, and buyers having surveys done then dropping out.

Silvia had had enough of estate agents so decided to put her own ad in the local paper – after all she was in advertising. It resulted in 5 enquiries and one no show after they had driven 30 miles to get home on time to meet them.

Frustrated they let the owners know they still didn't have a buyer and were told they could wait no longer.

The following week their neighbour informed them that a woman had called at her house and asking was it still for sale. She'd left her number so Silvia called her. They were interested and it turned out to be the buyers who never showed. They liked the house, had a mortgage in place and made them an offer. Silvia rang the owners to see if the house was still available and were told it wasn't.

This time Silvia was not going to start looking again until everything was moving and close to completion. She'd move into a hotel and put the furniture into storage if she had to.

Everything was going swimmingly until the buyers rang to say their solicitor said it would take a week to do the land searches. Silvia informed them their solicitor said it only takes 48 hours. The buyers started to make threats of pulling out. Silvia's land searches came back in 24 hours and called the buyers to inform them. They started making demands that Silvia move out by a certain date because her mother was coming over from New Zealand to stay with them and she needed to redecorate.
"I can't possibly move that week," Silvia told them, "Gorgeous is working away and I'll be on my own. You can't possibly expect me to move on my own, and you haven't even signed the forms yet so it might not be possible."

That weekend Silvia received a phone call but couldn't reach it in time so the answer machine picked up. A drunken voice at the other end just said "WANKER" and hung up. Silvia dialled 1471 and knew the number instantly. It was the buyers.

On Monday morning Silvia's solicitors made an application to see Draft Documents for the sale only to be told they had pulled out, then received a phone call from the buyers apologising and that they were still interested as all the paperwork was now done.

Silvia was annoyed but waited until they had signed before they started looking for a new house themselves. Gorgeous made the final decision after they whittled it down to the best of 2.

7 weeks later they were sitting in their living room with the van loaded outside and waiting for the funds to be transferred. They awaited their solicitor's call but it was lunchtime. The phone had been disconnected and they clutched the mobile in anticipation. At 2pm they were on their way to their new home.

Bloody stress and relax.

Several months later her old next door neighbour rang to say that the couple that had bought their old house had split up. She'd gone back to New Zealand after he'd lost his job so they were selling the house but not before he had got a job as a taxi driver and left the window open one night when he went out on a call and returned to find he'd been burgled.

Karma.

LES VACANCES

The French class had 15 minutes in which to retrieve a cup of coffee (that had the temperature of the surface of a dying planet) from a machine, drink it without doing oneself an injury and try to continue to speak French afterwards with a scorched tongue and blistered gums.

Silvia struggled with her grammar. It was so confusing trying to work out the difference between a passé compose and l'imparfait, let alone the conditional and subjunctive. The teacher explained it to her over and over again. She could feel the cogs in her brain grinding together like a dry engine gasping for lubrication, but they just wouldn't connect. She felt frustrated and stupid. It was a total immersion class and Silvia was drowning. All the others in the group seemed to grasp it more easily but they'd all been taught grammar in high school and knew how to conjugate a verb and split an infinitive. Silvia was totally out of her depth and feared her dream may never come to fruition.

She was sick of the rain in Manchester, every day driving towards the darker sky that always seemed to cover the city, even when it had been bright sunshine just a few minutes earlier when she'd left home.

She was fed up of sitting in stationary traffic every night on her way home, following the red snake rearing its head to strike, break light after break light creating a meander of colour as far as the eye could see, as she crawled the twelve miles to Exit 11 on the M62 where she could pull off and speed up to 40mph as she hit the slip road.

Utterly frustrated with her situation she surfed the pre-programmed, local radio stations in search of traffic news.

"Nothing, absolutely nothing, that means it's some stupid person driving at 50 miles an hour in the middle lane and won't get out of the way!" she fumed, under her breath.

She'd seen it so many times before, everyone happily motoring along at a steady 70mph then suddenly the red snake appears and everything grinds to a halt for no apparent reason. No accidents, no wide loads to manoeuvre past, no aircraft landing on the motorway, no UFO's buzzing the juggernauts, then there it is that old banger with the stubborn driver refusing to let anyone past, some sick revenge perhaps for everyone having a better car than him.

She'd already written to Salford Council to complain about the narrowing of the road at the end of the M602. Liverpool Street used to be a dual carriageway of sorts, until the council decided to add a cycle lane and paint chevrons down the middle of the road. This caused further bottlenecks and added another 10 minutes to her journey.

Her letter stated that if the council had thought it through properly they could open a third lane on the M602 by using the hard shoulder during rush hour to ease the traffic, they could have then painted the cycle lane on the seldom used pavements for extra safety and left two perfectly good traffic lanes to ease the congestion even more.

They wrote back saying the Emergency Services needed to use the hard shoulder and the cyclists would be safer on the road than on the pavement!

They also said the government were trying to encourage people to use public transport to ease congestion on our roads.

"Well if we had any bloody public transport that would be great," fumed Silvia, "but you cut out loads of trains or cancelled them, so people had no choice but to drive!"

She wrote back, "That's all very well," Silvia informed them, "but from where I live there are only two trains in the morning and to return there's one at 5.30pm and the next one is now at 7pm if you miss it, and as I don't finish work till 5.30pm I'd be hard pushed to catch that one unless I used the transporter room from the Star Ship Enterprise, and I'll be damned if I'm going to hang around a train station in the middle of winter for an hour and a half waiting for the next one, as it's usually cancelled anyway with the 'wrong snow' on the line, as it has to climb its way back over the Pennines from its trip to Scarborough. Why do you think I chose to drive in the first place? Because I like to get home at night, that's why and as for cycling, I'd have legs like a Russian shot putter!"

She was bored of her job in advertising, which didn't reap many rewards when compared to the amount of scolding she received from irate clients, a strange collection of individuals, who flew off the handle before assessing the facts. Silvia would explain the situation, they would realise their mistake, calm down but never, ever apologise.

She'd had enough of working for a living but couldn't think of a good enough reason to stop. Most women had babies and packed in work or took up to a year off to recover, but Silvia didn't want babies, she wanted a quiet life, free from screaming kids but exciting and full of surprises. She wanted to travel the world but had to do it in two-week intervals and carry on working to pay for everything. The women with kids used to moan that they wished they could do the same and how lucky Silvia was. They did have a choice and they'd made theirs.

This was her life not some kid's and from what she heard from other mums they were run ragged by their children's' demands for the latest products they saw on TV and kept in expensive clothes by their aspiring parents so as not to lower the tone of the neighbourhood. They were basically working their arses off and getting into debt to keep up with the latest gadgets and technology.

Silvia needed a holiday and a friend came up with an offer she couldn't refuse. Hilby had a cousin who lived in a petit hamlet in Brittany and she knew of a gite they could have for next to nothing. In fact, it was for nothing. All they had to do was find their ferry fare, petrol money and a French dictionary. An adventure was in the making.

Silvia researched the price of the ferry for a car and 4 people - Nel, Hilby's friend was coming too as there was plenty of room in the gite to sleep up to 6 - work out the nearest route they needed to take, (Portsmouth - St. Malo overnight with cabins) how long it would take to drive there, (4 hours) what was the best timed ferry they could make on a Saturday (6pm), plot the routes, (Warrington to Portsmouth and St. Malo to Josselyn) £400 return, book and pay.

Silvia decided that she couldn't possibly go without learning a little of the lingo first. She'd been on a few long weekends to Barcelona and Nice and had felt a complete prat when she couldn't ask for the simplest of things in their lingo. No, if she was going to do this she was going to do it properly. She enrolled at the local Alliance Francais and began the toughest learning period of her life. Her teacher was from Lyon, a native, and had the patience of a saint (unlike those at school who just left her to fend for herself when she couldn't keep up) you could almost see the stigmata in her palms.

For 3 hours, one night a week, for 8 months she swotted and fretted, studied and sweated and then it was September - time to Allez!

Gorgeous was designated the long distance driver but they would take Silvia's car as it was a big, spacious saloon and more comfortable with four of them and the boot could easily accommodate the entire luggage.

Essentials were purchased, like tea, coffee and chocolate, they were told NOT to take English toilet rolls as they block up the fosse, no need to buy wine it was cheaper in France. They stuffed casual, slobbing about clothes into a holdall each, this was going to be a relaxing time of BBQ-ing on the back patio, drinking the local Kir and generally mulling about the scenery in flat pumps and chinos, so no need for dressy clobber here.

With the boot stuffed full of gear Silvia and the holiday crew set off for the ferry with their passports, spectacles, testicles, wallets and watches, clean knickers and a French dictionary tucked under their belts. They settled into their overnight cabin and the ferry sailed into the English Channel/La Manche.

The crossing from Portsmouth to St. Malo was force six, which wasn't unnervingly rough but enough to make them all look drunk as they wandered the corridors, ricocheting off the walls, looking for the bar. She checked Gorgeous had taken his seasickness pills, which were now working a treat since they had switched brands. A disco blurted out from a corner. They took a balcony seat and ordered cocktails to celebrate the first night of their holiday. In their minds they were on a cruise ship and had just finished dining with the Captain.

By midnight they were beginning to feel the effects of their journey and decided to turn in for the night. By this time the ship was rolling from side to side and as quick as they got one leg in their bunks they were hopping backwards out of it again. Eventually, with the rock-a-by-baby effect of no stabilisers, they fell into the deep slumber only un enfant knows.

The next morning they awoke to the announcement that they were about to dock and disembarkment would be in an hour. A quick shower and change of clothes in calmer waters this time, restored the equilibrium and then time for a hearty breakfast of the fried variety to set them up for the two-hour drive ahead.

The view of St. Malo from the deck was a magnificent sight. An ancient granite-walled town of cobbled streets and turrets with twinkling windows as the early morning sun hit the glass. Boats of all sizes bobbed on the surf kicked up by the ferries reverse thrust. The smell of salty air and sun tan lotion filled their nostrils. It was 8am on a September morning and there were people already staking their claim on patches of golden sand.

"We could stay here on our last night," Silvia suggested. "It would save us having to leave La Cambout in the early hours to catch the ferry home."
"Great idea," answered Hilby. "Let's stop off at the tourist information and see what they have available."
"The place should be empty at this time of year, all the kids have gone back to school, so it shouldn't be a problem." Silvia reflected.

They picked up a brochure and scoured the pages for a cheap place to stay for one night's B&B. The Hotel Port Malo was just the place. At 11euros including croissants, bread, jam and coffee for le petit dejeuner and an en-suite room what more could they ask for? With the aid of le dictionnaire Silvia reserved deux chambres and went to explore the town.

It was as though time had stood still for centuries, the facades of buildings had remained the same, the roads were original or certainly looked that way, no local council had torn down their heritage here and replaced it with 1960's concrete blocks, it remained as pretty as a picture within the intra-muros (walls). Yet it had all the necessary requirements a town needs to feed and clothe its people. They would have to come back and spend a full day here before they left for home again.

Heading south-west towards Josselyn they stopped at Moncontour to stock up on supplies. A pretty little village of grey stone and baskets spilling geraniums with only a traditional local bar and supermarket open on this bright Dimanche morning. Un café grand was urgently required along with a loo stop. Le monsieur obliged with four huge mugs and gesticulated to a wooden door at the end of the room. A quick supermarket dash, "Don't forget the bread," said Hilby, and the car was packed even higher and off they went again - not far now.

Twenty minutes later they arrived at Le Bourgeoreille and raced around looking for the best bedrooms. There were three to choose from. Food was quickly packed into the fridge and cupboards and clothes hung up to de-crease. The kettle was on, the tea was brewed, the feet were up on the sofa and the biscuits were dunked to the rhythm of a slow waltz - ahh, relaxation.

"Right, let's go into town," said Silvia, excitedly, and they were off driving through the forest, spotting wild boar and deer, over the canal and heading for Josselyn.

It was a small, quaint village but well served with bars, restaurants and shops. The road opened into a square and wound down to the river. A small bridge crossing to the other side was covered in an assortment of flowering geraniums in pinks and reds. It was September but still hot enough to colour the skin.

There was a bar on the water's edge so they sat al fresco and ordered the local tipple, Kir. With the sun and a smile on their faces they took in the view of the chateau and watched the locals go about their business.

They decided to eat in that night and use some of the supplies that they had bought in Moncontour. Chicken, fresh vegetables, roast potatoes with lashings of gravy - no wonder the French call the English Les Roast Beefs being fond of a traditional Sunday roast, (only theirs was chicken). It had been another long day and after a suitable time to digest their fayre they retired for the evening.

Silvia's dictionnaire came in very handy. Whenever they went into a restaurant, and whenever Silvia's memory was stuck she quickly whipped it out under the tablecloth and looked up the offending word so she was ready for le serveur when he returned to take their order.

Dividing the county into four quarters, and hurtling down country roads with Hilby and Nel being bounced around in the back of the car, they explored each one thoroughly from Dinan with its steep winding lanes down to the river and the need of an iron lung to get back to the top again, to Vannes with its castle and pretty cobbled town, from coastline resorts with promenades to walk, to canals with weirs and colourful boats, and Mont St. Michel island with it's tourist shops and restaurants and a day off to rest and cook at home and make bread and butter pudding out of stale bread and left over fruit and eggs. Every time they went to the supermarche Hilby asked, "Do we need bread?" so they had to use it up somehow. Nothing was wasted.

Then it swiftly came to an end. After checking out of their gite they headed back to St. Malo to spend their last full day and night there before they sailed for Portsmouth the following morning.

The hotel rooms were above a bar playing loud music with the reception to one side.

"Great, a bit of life," said Hilby, but I don't know about those stairs! She looked ahead at a set of steps tucked away in the corner that spiralled upwards into darkness.

"It'll be fine," reassured Silvia, knowing how nervous Hilby could be at times and flicked a switch so a light came on to guide their way.

They climbed up to their rooms on the third floor and slung their overnight bags on to the beds. The building was tall and narrow with only three rooms on each level. The window overlooked a cobbled street 40 feet below and if you cricked your neck far enough you could see the outer walls of the town and then the sea. A quick wash of faces and they descended the helter-skelter stairs and spilled onto the street to look for the entrance that would lead them onto the top of the wall.

It was like a mini version of the Great Wall of China with four different views of north, south, east and west, each showing a different section of the town. From nuns playing rounders, to hoteliers setting up for evening diners. It was still a warm summer evening but the wind blew strong on top of the wall. After completing one circuit they descended down onto the cobbles again. All hungry now, it was time to do some last minute shopping and find a little place to eat.

The town was a labyrinth of tiny streets and squares and as dusk fell turned into twinkling sparkles of light. They entered one of the squares and smelt the exotic aroma of blended spices wafting from the door of a Moroccan restaurant. The proprietor welcomed them and showed them to a table where he prepared mint tea while they waited for their couscous.

A magnificent dish arrived from the kitchen with stewed meats and vegetables of several kinds. A most satisfying feast and a contented stomach, well at least until breakfast.

There were shops and restaurants of every kind. From speciality cake shops, wine caves and perfumeries producing their own brands. The air hung heavy with scent as they passed the doorways, tempting them to go inside. Laden with packages they returned to their tower to offload and ventured back out to find a watering hole. Safely tucked away in a dark corner of a music bar they ordered the local beer and spied on the passing trade.

They watched revellers of all shapes and sizes, hen parties from Jersey, you name it, they passed through the bar. Suitably relaxed and slightly intoxicated they returned to their tower for a full night's sleep before their departure for the ferry the following morning.

About 4am Silvia was woken by a steady and continuous squeaking noise. The kind bedsprings make when a couple are enjoying the steady rhythm of passion.
"Lucky bastards," she thought and turned over trying to ignore it.
An hour later and it was still going on.
"Bloody hell, she must have Casanova up there, lucky bitch."
An hour later he was still going strong.
"This can't be right," Silvia muttered in a daze. "Even a passionate Latin lover can't last that long."

She stumbled out of bed, passing the window and noticed the wind was howling outside.
"Not a good day for a ferry ride if it's rough," she worried for Gorgeous and the seasickness and Hilby not yet having found her sea legs. When she pressed her nose against the glass she realised that the squeaking noise stopped, the squeaking was actually coming from the old French windows in their room. The wind pushing them from outside was causing the metal fastenings to rock back and forth in its holder causing friction. She shoved some tourist info leaflets into the

gap, which promptly stopped the noise, and satisfied with her solution, she happily climbed back into bed.

After a somewhat disturbed and sleepless night she picked up the telephone and ordered le petit dejeuner from the bar.
"Cinq minutes, s'il vous plait," the proprietor informed her.
Two cups of strong coffee, croissants and confiture later she was ready to roll on and roll off the ferry back in Angleterre. They'd had a wonderful, stress-free week exploring Britanny and after her much earned break to northern France, Silvia realised what she had been missing all those years she'd spent holidaying in Spain and Greece - tranquility.

Her plan was put into action, she would continue to learn French, buy a gite and go and live in France. She longed for the sun on her skin, penetrating deep into her, to remove the dampness from her bones. Every time she went on holiday her skin had to turn from blue to the normal white of les Anglaises first, then to pink to red and finally to a light brown that she could proudly call a tan.

Back in Manchester she enrolled for the next French course and scoured the Internet for properties for sale in Josselyn and dreamed of the day she could afford one and go.

IT ISN'T CHRISTMAS, IT'S JUST WEDNESDAY

Ah, Christmas, 'tis that joyous time of year when Silvia makes friends with all those around her she has found frustratingly annoying for the last 11 months. December is the time for making amends, granting forgiveness, cramming in as many parties as she can and clearing off the cobwebs before she begins the onslaught of dreary January with only the sales to keep her going.

"Two months in the planning all for a day that lasts a few hours and constitutes a meal no better than her Mother's usual Sunday roast. Then everybody goes home and leaves you to admire your presents, do the dishes and clean up all the discarded wrapping paper and bows for recycling onto next year's gifts," she pondered, bemused.

It's October pay day, when the not so big fat cheque goes in the bank account and Silvia feels more generous than usual. That weekend is when she starts her treasure hunt for suitable gifts for the ever-growing list of relatives and friends.

"What can I buy my mum?" Silvia asks Gorgeous. "She has all the Nao collection from years of travelling to Spain. She doesn't wear much perfume and has enough bottles of it anyway to stock a Fragonard back catalogue. As for jewellery she's allergic to everything but gold and has more earrings than a gypsy fortune teller and if she wears anymore necklaces at the same time she'll look like Mr. T and start walking with a stoop!"
"How about a black leather bag?" came the reply from Gorgeous.
"I got her one last year," replied Silvia.
"You can never have too many bags. Like shoes really, you always say," he quipped.
"Dad's OK to buy for - golf or painting implements and he's happy as Larry and my brother, he's so difficult to buy for, too. Will only wear crew neck sweaters, doesn't like clothes generally, only ever see him in Fire Brigade sweats or a T-shirt if it's warm. I don't think he wears

aftershave. As for an earring he could borrow some of my mum's," Silvia laughed. "Perhaps it's a Capricorn thing like having possession of the remote control for the TV," she slyly dug.

Then there's Gorgeous's side of the family – 3 sisters, 1 brother, 2 brothers-in-law, 1 sister-in-law, 5 nieces, 3 nephews, 10 babies and a partridge in a pear tree. They all have presents and a table gift as well! So that's another few hundred quid to allow for. Tons of wrapping paper, tissue paper, gift bags and bows, tying labels on to them all so they know who the gifts are from, the spare room looks like Santa crash landed and left a couple of sacks behind.

Silvia's joints were sore from kneeling down for hours wrapping and writing labels and stacking them in piles around the room in date order of when the exchange of presents was to take place. Something that can't all be done on the same day and is staggered throughout December according to the various relatives calendars to make themselves available, which is prone to change at the drop of a hat because one in particular always double books without checking with anyone else's plans first.

Silvia's dining table was just too small for this job and was reserved for the writing of Christmas cards and was already piled high with boxes of cards from various stores (donations to charities by purchasing a box, of course) and card shops (more in a box).

Silvia began the task of writing more than 100 cards and checked her list of labels for those who have moved house throughout the year, split up from their partners and now require their own separate ones, and those who now have new partners or who have remarried and changed their names. Every year she vowed to get the list down to a more manageable size but it always seemed to keep expanding.

One year she decided to deviate from her usual ritual of posting everyone's cards on 30th November so they arrived on 1st December to kick start Christmas - and to free up some room on the dining table so they can eat there again - and decided not to post them or even write them until she received one herself and would return one on the same day to that person. If any dropped out she would save a lot of time, effort and money! That year they received over 100 cards – so that plan didn't work.

As she went through her list Silvia spotted some names that brought a lump to her throat, those that had passed away so quickly and unexpectedly, those who had died slowly and in a lot of pain, memories came flooding back and with sadness she crossed their names off the list, only to send the card to their surviving partners. It was reminiscent of two of her cousins.

"Do we cry in self-pity or the hopelessness of the situation in which we find ourselves?" she asked Gorgeous. "The mere fact that we are helpless to ease the passage from one life to another is enough to cause us endless anxiety. Why does it have to be so painful on both parts? The deterioration of the body, like the soul stripping off the layers to get out. No longer needing the ailing vehicle in which it is travelling. And for those who watch and wait, not wanting them to suffer but not wanting them to leave. The indecision, the uselessness, and the indignity of it all," she asked, but there was no answer.

Carol had suffered for 4 years. She'd discovered a lump in her breast and promptly went to get it investigated. When nothing showed up on a mammogram she assumed all was well and forgot about it. Two years later she had a scan because the lump was still there and starting to give her some trouble. That's when they discovered it. Cancer with a capital "C".

She told them to take the breast off and they said it was too drastic, they'd only need to remove the lump, give her some radiotherapy and she'd be right as rain.

Carol returned to work in the bingo hall, which she loved, and carried on looking after her daughter, she needed to work because it paid the mortgage. Her two sons from a previous marriage had grown up and had families of their own. Her partner had become distant and she found some dodgy CDs he'd downloaded from the Internet. She gave him an ultimatum. He chose the porn. She kicked him out.

He thought he could get her to pay half his debts but she told him he should have married her and then she might have been liable, but as he'd refused and they weren't married, the debt was all his.

They sold the house and she bought another one, an old council house that had been previously occupied by a pensioner and needed a total refurbishment. She began to ache and thought she'd overdone it with the decorating. She mentioned it to the consultant on her next visit. He dismissed it as nothing but took some X-rays to monitor the situation. When she went back for her results they were waiting at the hospital door for her with a wheelchair.

The X-ray had revealed a fracture of the femur, they didn't know how she was still standing, and the strength of the muscle was the only thing that was keeping her upright.

They wheeled her into the consultant and he explained that she would have to have a steel rod inserted into her leg. The operation went well but the rod was too long and shattered her kneecap. They took her down again and put a shorter one in. She spent weeks recovering. Once a month she had to return to have some magic liquid pumped into her to 'coat the bones'. This used to make her hands bleed where the needle was inserted, oozing out of her nails and skin. She mentioned it to the nurse.

"Oh, I've never seen anything like that before," she said, and walked away.

But the dull ache in her leg never went away.

She kept mentioning it to the doctor and the consultants but they said, "Of course it aches you have steel rod in there!" Like it was the most natural thing in the world. "Just take painkillers," they said, "and try to stay off it."

Work was good to her and let her change her job to a more sedentary one as a number caller, but it never seemed to help. At home she spent most of her time sitting with her feet up on the sofa and a blanket wrapped around her. She found it difficult to get up the stairs and fell down them once.

She lost her appetite and couldn't eat anything, and brought it back up when she did. Silvia's Mother sent Silvia round with a few cans of rice pudding to see if the soothing warm nectar would help. It did for a while. Carol turned to Silvia and said, "I don't want to end up like our Keith."

Keith, their cousin, had a pain in his chest and had been for an X-ray but while he waited for the results a lump appeared in his neck. All weekend he fiddled with it until his girlfriend (at the time and there were many) insisted that he get it looked at and dragged him to A&E at Arrowe Park for an examination.

They retrieved his X-ray for analysis. The news he received wasn't good. He had a growth in his chest so big that it was impossible to operate on because it was so near to his heart. They removed the lump in his neck and he began 6 months of chemo. The tumour in his chest shrunk significantly small enough to be removed by scraping it away from his heart.

His long, dark, shiny hair he'd always tied back in a ponytail had been reduced to a fuzz on his scalp. He could have given Yul Brynner a run for his money. No eyebrows and no eyelashes but he still had hairy legs! His scar looked like a shark attack bite along the line of his right rib cage front to back. He sat proudly on his bed bear-chested showing his battle wounds with death.

He was off work for 12 months but being as fit as a butcher's dog he made a good recovery and was all set to return to work (building wings for aeroplanes - although how he switched to that from hairdressing Silvia never knew - and DJing in his spare time) when he went for his final scan.

There was a shadow. He'd need another op to remove part of his lung. "But you can still lead a normal life," they told him, "as part of it grows back again to compensate."

It was April. He started his next course of chemo and 6 months passed again. By October he was having difficulty writing cheques and signing his name. He started to lose his memory and couldn't recognise his friends. He stayed with his mum and dad because he could no longer live on his own. One morning they couldn't wake him and they called the hospital.

The hospital was worried and did a brain scan and found a tumour. They said there was nothing more they could do, then changed their minds. He'd have to have it removed and transferred him to Fazakerley Hospital where they examined his scan and the surgeon discovered 4 tumours not one!
"It's inoperable," they told him. "We could have removed one but not 4."

"How in God's name, can you miss 3 tumours and build someone's hopes up in this way?" Silvia remarked, incredulously. She was shocked, after everything he'd been through, the chemo, the ops, the dashed hopes, the shattered dreams for the future.

His friends organised a fundraiser for him to help pay his mortgage, as he didn't have any critical illness insurance. He could lose his house while he waited to die. They discussed sending him to America where he might get treatment. Then the fits started and they knew it was too late for him to travel the distance.

They sent him back to St. John's hospice and gave him radiotherapy to make it more comfortable for him. He asked them, "How long have I got?"
"1-7 months," they said.

The last time Silvia saw him in Clatterbridge, he had the dark eyelids of death and she knew it wouldn't be long but she hoped for a miracle anyway.
"Is the miracle for us?" she asked herself, "or them. Is the miracle actually 'death' so they no longer suffer?"

There was just the family around the bed that Sunday night and as Silvia talked to his Father, who always had a million and one questions, Silvia heard Keith ask his mum, "Does she know?"
"Yes, she knows son."

Silvia wanted to hold his hand but couldn't get near enough; she could hardly look at him in case she cried. Crying was not allowed at the deathbed. He was always amazed that she had travelled so far to see him as he thought it was a long way away, on another planet not 30 miles. Silvia wanted to tell him he was loved to make sure he knew, but couldn't bring herself to say it in front of the others.

It was October and he died in November - 1 month later but 7 months after they found the shadow. How ironic.

The chapel at Landican crematorium was packed solid. They put up speakers outside so those who couldn't get in could hear the tributes. Silvia stood outside, thankful that she had missed the coffin arriving and for fear of breaking down. She was always late and wondered if she'd be late for her own funeral. She hated seeing the coffin disappearing behind the curtains, for she believed that they were still with you until that very moment.

Silvia didn't recognise the person they described in their eulogies, this happy-go-lucky man who never held a grudge.
"So unlike the rest of us," she thought. "He even stayed friends with all his ex-girlfriends and wives!"
The things he'd done in his life. He'd lived everyday to the full. There was no time to stay angry it was all about love and life and living it. Dance like your life depended on it, because tomorrow you may not be able to.
"Perhaps deep down in his subconscious he knew there wasn't going to be much time for trivialities and had to fit a lifetime into 46 years."

Why did he die so young? Because God needed a DJ for a party he was throwing. If only we knew the answer then maybe we could accept the fact why people die, why loved ones are taken away from us, why people suffer.

Why?...Because…Oh, OK then.

***

"What have they told you?" Silvia asked Carol, concerned.

"I asked the McMillan nurse how long I had, and she said it's usually 4 years from diagnosis."

Silvia sat and looked at her in stunned silence.

"So have they actually said what it is you have, have they confirmed it?"

"No, I'm still waiting for them to see me."

Every month she went for her magic liquid she complained about the pain again and insisted they investigate. For months they did nothing but eventually set up an MRI scan under duress. By this time 9 months had passed. That's when they told her "matter-of-factly" and without a compassionate bedside manner, "Oh yes, it's cancer."

Carol came out in a daze. She didn't know what had hit her. She'd been on at them for months and they did nothing and now they tell her this. For two years she'd had breast cancer, and they hadn't been bothered to check her further.

Some patients get offered chemo - Carol was offered nothing. They scanned her and discovered it had spread to the rib, hip and spine and found another lump in her other breast and they did nothing about that either. It was always the same. Their treatment of her was diabolical. The surgeon told her to give up her job. She told them she had a mortgage to pay. He said, "The mortgage is the least of your worries."

Work told her to take all the time she needed, they would keep her job open for her. She really loved it there.

She asked the surgeon if he was going to remove the breast. He told her they were more concerned about the other areas first. Her case notes read "TERMINAL". Then the headaches started. A scan showed a tumour on the pituitary gland. They zapped it with radiotherapy and upped her medication. It did nothing.

She stayed at her Mother's house for a few weeks to rest and be looked after. She hardly got out of bed. She tried to sit in the sunshine but was restless and went back to bed. They took her for a walk along the promenade but she was so tired.

Then one morning Joan couldn't wake her. They called the doctor and she diagnosed pneumonia and rushed her into hospital. Her sodium levels were so high she was at risk of having a massive heart attack. She had to remain on a normal ward, as the hospice wouldn't take her in case she infected the other patients. Like it was going to make a difference - they were dying anyway and hospital acquired pneumonia was always rife.

By this time Silvia knew she was going too, but she still prayed for that miracle.

They fed Carol a cocktail of 17 pills everyday. If she could walk she would rattle. They even had her on anti-depressants. Nothing worked so they withdrew all medication. Her case notes read "TLC – TENDER, LOVING CARE".

Then a miracle happened. The pneumonia cleared and the sodium levels returned to near normal and Carol recovered enough to be sitting in the chair when Silvia went to see her. She had a nebulizer strapped round her face and all the family were sitting around the room. It was Sunday 3rd July.

The nurse came in and told her they had found a bed on the ward and she didn't have to be in a room on her own anymore. She could pick which one out of two she preferred and they would move her out that evening.

On Tuesday 5th July Carol relapsed with a blood clot in her leg. They put her back in the side room and still didn't offer her any medication. On Saturday 9th July Silvia went to see her again. The door to her room was shut and the curtain across the small window was drawn. She tapped lightly on the door not knowing what she would find on the other side. She took a deep breath to prepare herself and turned the handle. She pushed the door open and saw Carol's ex-husband, his sister and her husband, Carol's son and her best friend sitting at the side of her bed, the TV was on and Carol continued to stare at the film now playing.

There was no sign of the ex-boyfriend of 3 years; he obviously still preferred to download porn than hospital visiting.

The small room couldn't hold all of them so all but her friend left to get some refreshments in the hospital café. While they were gone Silvia sat on the other side of the bed and stroked Carol's hair, sending her healing and praying once more for a miracle. She soaked little sponges on the end of sticks in water that looked like lollipops and ran them over her dry and cracked lips.

Carol lifted the bedclothes and showed Silvia her leg, now twice its original size. She was in pain and every breath hurt her chest. She kept catching it and holding her hand to it as if her heart would give out at any moment. Silvia's eyes filled with tears and she fought to hold them back. Carol pressed the buzzer and asked the nurse for a painkiller. She went to get someone else; someone authorized to dish out the morphine.

The medicater came in with a small pill and a smug look on her face and checked Carol's chart. She must have seen this scene a thousand times and had become acclimatised to it. She asked her her name and her date of birth. Carol could hardly get the words out she was so weak.

"Just give her the bloody pill," Silvia thought to herself as the Smug Medicater held out her hand.

When the eyelids look dark and the once brilliant white teeth now discoloured and brown like they'd seen a thousand cups of strong, black coffee and held a million cigarettes between them but never paid a visit to the dentist, Silvia knew it wouldn't be long now. They say you get better just before you die - it gives all those around you, watching and waiting, a false hope.

Silvia had called to say goodbye. She didn't utter her usual parting message "I'll see you soon"; because she knew it would have been a lie. Carol's friend ordered her, "Don't you go anywhere until Tuesday because I can't get back to the hospital till then."

Silvia brushed Carol's hair with her hand and kissed her on the forehead. She was clammy and just kept staring at the TV. She sent her healing to help her journey become less painful, almost giving her permission to go. Carol never wanted to die; they'd both watched Keith die in a similar way.
"I don't want to die like Keith did," she'd said with the saddest look on her face, remembering the suffering he went through with his brain tumour and the fits, she wanted to watch her kids and grandchildren grow.

For two years she'd had cancer and didn't know it. She'd asked a Macmillan nurse "How long do people usually live with this?"
The answer had come back 1-4 years. She thought she had at least this and had booked a holiday. She would be away at the same time as Silvia, the 11th July, Silvia was leaving on the 10th but they were going in opposite directions. Carol preferred a cooler climate and had booked a cruise to Norway. Silvia hated the cold and booked a sunshine holiday to Ischia, where Gorgeous's family were from. But it was already too late.

Silvia closed the door to Carol's room and headed out of the ward. She met the rest of the family coming back and filled with emotion, burst into tears at the injustice of it all.

Silvia left for Italy the next day. On her first night there she was woken in the early hours by three loud thunderclaps. She lifted her head off her pillow and looked around the room. The dawn was starting to creep through the slats on the shuttered French windows. Silvia spoke into the darkness, "Are you going now love? OK then," and fell back asleep.

The next morning while they were getting ready to go to the beach Gorgeous checked his phone messages. Suddenly Silvia felt his arms tighten around her and wondered what he was playing at this early in the day, he whispered in her ear, "She's gone, love. She passed away in the early hours of this morning." It didn't register what he was saying at first, she thought he was getting fresh, then her eyes filled with tears and her face contorted with the pain of heartbreak. Was the previous night's thunderclaps Carol's way of letting her know she was going?

Silvia phoned her Mother and she'd said she had looked at the picture of her own Mother she kept on top of the TV and said "Olly, get the kettle on, you've got a visitor coming."

How cruel to take her away. What could she be wanted for in this other place that was more important than here? This other place, where Keith had gone to DJ only 8 months before.

The day she died was 4 years from when she first discovered the lump. The day she died should have been the day she sailed to Norway on her cruise. It seems she got her holiday after all.

***

Everybody panics, as Christmas Day gets nearer. Anxiety levels increase. Charity and Samaritans ads start appearing on the bottom of the TV screens. Christmas is a joyous time of year but for some it can be the worst day of the year.

"Why don't they recondition themselves into a different way of thinking about it, to get through it?" Silvia thought. "I know it's tough and we've all had problems, breakups, and utter feelings of complete loneliness at times in our lives, but most of us manage to pull through and cope - why is it that some of us can and some of us can't?" she questioned.

"Why don't they think of it as just another day like any other day, except that you are off work so it's a bit like a weekend. You have a Christmas dinner which is only a small step up from the usual Sunday roast except you get pigs in blankets as a bonus and exchange gifts (so a bit like a birthday) that you probably don't want or need anyway. If people are on their own why don't they buy themselves a nice present, a treat, something they have always wanted that no one else would think to buy them and present it to themselves on Christmas morning! That way they could enjoy something to take their minds off their problems or worries even if only for a short while. Why they could even buy themselves a holiday so they have something to look forward to!" she said with a smile. "In fact, that's such a good idea, I might do that myself in future so at least we can plan what we are going to do when we get there, over Christmas, after everyone has gone," she said happily.

"Everyone assumes that everyone else is having such a good time with those they love around them, but that's not always the case. Husband's hate their Mothers-in-law arriving for the season and interfering, and moan it's the only time they have off work. Wives hate their Mothers-in-law staying and completely taking over, because they consider them opinionated (why don't you do it like this – I don't make my gravy like that), everyone is putting on a brave face trying to get through it without having an argument," she answered herself.

"If people are alone at Christmas is it because they really don't want to be bothered with anyone else? They prefer their own company but panic a little as the time draws closer and think that they are not normal and maybe should be doing what everyone else is doing. Or is it because they really do want to be on their own, honestly, they've seen it all before year after year and are fed up to the back teeth with it all and just want some peace and quiet?" Silvia pondered.

Silvia's friend April informed her that this year as she didn't have a husband, a boyfriend, parents or relatives around to annoy her she was going to lock the front door, stay in her pyjamas and watch TV all day, slumped on the sofa and hopefully catch all of the Queen's speech and the Snowman without interruption, open a large box of Thornton's chocolates and think about nothing but the TV guide. Silvia thought this was a great idea – she'd yet to see either, as helpful Gorgeous's family always talked through every programme and movie with a running commentary. It must be the Italian in them.

"If people want company why don't they take a look down their own street and invite the old man or lady from next door around for an eggnog, they could be alone and cold in their own homes not being able to afford to put their heating on because they have no one to help with the costs. Their own kids might think it's too far for them to travel to see them or can't because of bad weather. Why not go and visit them or invite them into their own home for an hour or two. They might just make a new friend, someone who understands how lonely they feel themselves," April offered a solution.

"But then if they do turn out to be an old grumpy boots and do nothing but moan all day, then welcome to what the rest of us have to suffer each year. No we're not all having fun with the family - most of us would skip the moaning and arguing and bugger off to warmer climes to have a nice holiday with complete strangers if we could. So they might just be better off staying on their own and watching telly in peace and quite - or enjoy the heaven of watching a movie from start to finish with no unnecessary dialogue from a third party, or fourth or fifth!" Silvia told April.

Silvia decided she needed a little treat herself, a nice present to herself, something she'd always wanted but it was a bit too expensive to add to the weekly shopping list. She set off for King Street and Liberty's, she'd been in many times and admired their range of silk fabrics already cut and ready to be sewn into a posh skirt which she'd had in mind for a male friend's wedding, but when the invitation failed to arrive in time for the big day in May she knew something was amiss.

Josh had worked with Silvia for a few years and decided advertising wasn't for him. He wanted to go to Los Angeles to be noticed and earn his fortune, although what in was never made clear. He handed in his notice at the agency and with his Father's sponsorship decided to go and live in Los Angeles for 6 months but nothing extraordinary happened and on the flight back he sat next to a girl from the same village, they got talking, started dating and the next thing is the wedding date is set.

There was a huge buzz of excitement going round, he couldn't wait to tell everyone how wonderful everything is, but then nothing. March came and went, so did April but no invitation, which was now well past the etiquette for securing an outfit for the occasion. Twelve months passed and Silvia had moved agencies and was now working with the Cheshire set when a call came through from Josh.

"I'm so sorry," he offered. "I keep getting your Christmas cards and I never reply, I feel so awful." Silvia could hear dishes being washed in the background so she knew he was with someone.

"Had they decided to call off the wedding and just live together?" she wondered. "It wasn't unusual given all the pressure parents put on their children during marital arrangements."

After they had exchanged all their news and Silvia had discovered that he was now working in the Middle East for an oil company, Josh took the bravest step he had ever taken in his life.

"I've met someone," he confessed, "but it's the wrong sex."

He waited for the phone to go down and to hear the dialling tone, but Silvia just said, "Not for you Josh, I think we all always suspected but we were just waiting for you to let us know in your own time, I'm so happy for you, I'd rather see two people loving each other than fighting with each other - no matter what sex." The relief in his voice was immense. He knew he had a friend for life.

As she walked through the big glass doors of Liberty's the smell of pot purri was enticingly heavy with the scent of cinnamon and orange spice - perfect for making the house smell like Christmas. She picked up a bag with its posh gold label and tied with ribbon, it was marked with a price tag of £10, a bit expensive for Silvia's usual shopping habits and dried bits of wood shavings, but it was Christmas and this was supposed to be a treat.

She turned to head towards the till and noticed that the shop was in disarray as they were already preparing for the January Sales. There were two staff sitting on the floor of the shop repricing silk scarves and refolding them, both ignored Silvia like she was invisible.

"I don't know what to do next," sighed one of them.

"You can serve me if you like!" piped up Silvia. "Bloody Sales Prevention Officers," she harrumphed under her breath, "they must be losing businesses thousands and it'll probably be half price tomorrow."

HAPPY NEW YEAR

Silvia awoke in a positive mood, which was very unusual as she always dreaded going back to work after the holidays. The drive in was almost pleasant - hardly any traffic, empty car park and a fairly dry morning. The car park attendant wished her a Happy New Year and proceeded to tell her how he was mugged for all his takings at another car park in the centre of Manchester and wasn't sure he wanted to be back at work. It wasn't the first time it had happened either. Oh, no, this was his second misfortune and he'd ended up in hospital for several days. All the time keeping the barrier down and prohibiting Silvia from driving off to park her car while he finished his story.

Silvia didn't want to appear rude and glanced at the clock on her dashboard. She'd purposely left the house 15 minutes early as part of her New Year's Resolution to get to work on time. As the minutes ticked by and her neck began to feel the strain of looking to the right for ten minutes without a break, she sighed inside.
"It's just not meant to be. I am just doomed from getting anywhere on time!" "I'm really sorry to hear that, it must have been very frightening for you," she offered, sympathetically, knowing full well how frightening it was from her own experience. Finally, the barrier lifted and she was off.

First job when arriving at work was fire up the server for any incoming emails, go to the loo and put the kettle on and make a nice cup of freshly brewed Columbian coffee, place home made, low-calorie sandwiches in the fridge and settle down to open the post and check the telephone messages.

"Not much work in for the morning so a pretty easy day ahead", she thought.

By the afternoon, people were chasing their jobs. So Silvia made the necessary phone calls to find out where everything was up to, only to be told by one printer that they had never received a certain file that her colleague had promised he'd send before Christmas! The job was now well overdue, the client was having a coronary and her credibility was swiftly sliding down a greasy pole.

"We'll get it to you today," she promised.

As soon as she replaced the receiver she put in a request for the missing files to be sent so the printer could start on them as soon as possible. Later that day they still hadn't been sent. She asked again.

"Who do you think you are?" came the reply from Ponsonby Smythe, waving his arms around imitating Bruce Lee's flails and screeching at her in a hysterical effeminate voice. "Sitting there like my Mother telling a 40-year old what to do!"

"If you acted like a 40-year old, I wouldn't have to," Silvia retorted. "It's my job as Production Manager to make sure that all jobs go out on time so I can make my delivery dates. If you had done it when you promised originally I wouldn't be nagging you now."

"Are you trying to make me look stupid?" he snapped back like a petulant child.

"You don't need any help from me in that department," Silvia fired back at him.

Silvia didn't sleep much that night. It was a difficult job at the best of times without having to battle with your own team. She knew she needed a lifestyle change but every time she applied for better paid jobs the answer always came back the same. *"Thank you for the interest you have shown in our company but due to the high standard of candidates we will not be taking your application further".*

If she did get an interview, it was always 'you're over qualified', 'not enough experience', 'too old', or the recruitment agencies would try to get you to go for a job you definitely knew wasn't suitable, just to reach their target that month.

She woke the next morning feeling a bit down and dragged her bum into the bathroom, stumbled downstairs in a half sleep for a bowl of cereal and a cup of tea and contemplated her future. She'd watched a programme on the TV about a couple who had relocated to France for a new life and wished she could do the same. Less poxy rain and bit more warmth in her bones.

She arrived at work late again to find her colleague had beaten her in and had already brewed the coffee. A kind of peace offering I suppose, to combat his guilt. Silvia accepted it with open palms, she was tired of fighting and Tina Turner sang in her head "It's time for letting go."

TECHNOPHOBE

Silvia hated computers. In fact she hated any type of technical item.
"They never do what you want them to," she protested, "five minutes
to type a letter and all morning to get the bleedin' thing to print out!"
Command Apple P
Menu says - how many?
One please
Sorry cannot recognise printer
"What do you mean? Look there it is," Silvia told the computer and
turned the screen around to face the printer, "see?" as though it had
eyes. Billy this bloody thing won't work again.
Billy the techno guy fixed it and gave her a book - Computers for
Dummies.

Not wanting to be defeated Silvia studied it alongside doing her job
and practised in her spare time at home. She really didn't know
enough about computers and they were beginning to take over the
world, she needed to find out all she could to keep her head above
water, so when she got to the end of the book she went on a college
course to get her ECDL (European Computer Driving Licence).

She went a few times a week in the evenings and when they were
quiet in work the boss let her have the time off to go and do another
module. Silvia couldn't believe it when she sat the exams - she was

passing them all with flying colours and marks over 90%. After 6 months she'd completed all the modules and exams and received a certificate in the style of a passport and a credit card - she felt important and was confident that she had more qualifications under her belt to get that next job she applied for.

Computers weren't the only things that freaked Silvia out. The TV remote was another item that Silvia just couldn't fathom out.
"So many buttons and why do you need more than one?" she asked Gorgeous, who was as good as a small child was with these things. Silvia puzzled over them.
"One's for the TV and one's for the box," Gorgeous said, informatively. "You have to switch both on and wait for the box to operate because it's like booting up a computer - it takes time," he instructed. He was a Capricorn. Silvia was impatient.

She remembered a time when you just turned the telly on and the picture was practically instant, nowadays you could go and make a cup of tea while you waited! Now if you changed channels there was a pregnant pause while it thought about it.

"If you want to set the timer to record anything you have to set the time, date, channel on this one and press the transfer button while pointing it at the TV and it will set it," he carried on his instructions.

Silvia tried it one night when he was out and managed to somehow put the child lock on it and couldn't get it off again so couldn't watch a thing all night. Gorgeous returned home to find every light on the box flashing on and off and it took him half an hour to get it unlocked and working again himself.

One evening Silvia came in from work while Gorgeous cooked the dinner. She sat on the sofa and picked up both remotes, exhausted.

"I need to figure this out," she said to herself, scratching her head, but after a few minutes of looking at each of them in turn, and trying to figure out, in her tired state, which one was for the TV and which one was for the box, Gorgeous walked in from the kitchen, took them out of her hands, turned to face the TV, pressed a few buttons till the picture came on, turned back to Silvia and placed them back in each of her hands and walked back out before she could say thanks or even realise what just happened.

THE GIFT HORSE

Silvia got a call from her Father demanding he come and see her. This was not a usual request, and had happened only once before.

Silvia's Mother had offered Silvia some money as a gift. Silvia didn't like to take their hard earned cash and refused to accept it saying she would rather her Mother went out and spent it on herself on a good holiday or some new clothes, and she had money of her own and didn't need it. Silvia's Mother had thrust it at Silvia saying "I've given the same to your brother so you have to take it." Silvia did, reluctantly.

A week later it was Mother's day. Silvia had written her a thank you note for the donation and apologised for her reluctance to take it but would use it towards her own holiday fund and said in future she would take anything that was given to her without putting up a fight.

Silvia's Mother had taken it the wrong way and got herself in a distressed state of mega proportions. Her Father had phoned the next day to ask for an explanation as to what the message meant because when her Mother had read it she had got upset.

It was written to mean that because her parents had brought her up to be independent and never ask for anything, and never take anything from anyone that Silvia found it hard to accept gifts, but thanks anyway, and she'll try not to put up such a fight in future and gladly take anything that's offered!

Silvia's Mother read it as meaning that in some way they had damaged and deprived her in her upbringing and now she was going to grab anything she could get and were thinking of changing their will!

After profuse apologies that it certainly wasn't meant that way and once everyone had wiped their tears, peace once again returned to the riverbank.

So when the call came this time Silvia paced anxiously up and down the living room, frequently glancing out of the window to watch for an approaching car.
"What have I done this time?" Silvia began, when he finally emerged from parking.
His eyes glistened with tears as he announced that after 48 years of marriage her parents were separating.

Silvia felt like she had been punched in the face. Surprisingly she remained calm and began the barrage of questions, Why? What? When? Where? How? And Who?
Why - because he no longer loved mum.
What - her drinking and the verbal abuse had forced him out of the house.
When - eventually after a few years he found solace is the arms of another.

Where - in the local pub where he used to meet his golfing and darts buddies.

How - through a circle of friends who met once a week after college art class and for the quiz night.

Who - a widow of 60 with 3 kids of her own.

Silvia's Mother didn't want him to leave, but he felt he didn't want to stay. She had given him the task of telling Silvia and her brother. It filled him with shame and guilt but he came anyway because he was worried that Silvia wouldn't want to see him again and that her brother might ban him from seeing his grandchildren.

Silvia's brother said he wasn't surprised. Mum had taken to drinking whisky and became verbally abusive towards dad when drunk, who wouldn't retaliate because he'd got past caring and therefore wasn't interested in taking her to get the help she needed. Silvia blamed him for that. That he could have done more to nip things in the bud but had always been a "yes" man.

Whatever mum had wanted, or recently not wanted to do, she wouldn't let dad do either and he never put up a fight. Silvia called it the "royal" we.

"We" wouldn't like that or it isn't "our" kind of thing," she said once when Silvia suggested they all go to Center Parcs together as a family. We could take it in turns to sit in one night each with the kids while the other two couples go out together and have a nice meal, talk some and generally relax.

"It isn't our kind of thing," she replied. Silvia looked at her Father and he never intervened, just lowered his eyes to the floor.

"Is that the Royal "we", then?" she asked them both. No answer. But she could tell he would have really liked to try it. They didn't go. Silvia never suggested anything again.

Well evidently it was dad's kind of thing and he felt compelled to go out and find someone else who liked doing the kind of things he did. How could Silvia blame him for not wanting to sit in the house for the rest of his days - waiting for death as he put it.

"I don't know how long I have got left," he told her, "but I want to enjoy it."

Silvia was surprised by her calmness and understanding. Maybe it hadn't hit her yet. She listened patiently while he went on about what a wonderful person he'd met, she was intelligent and made him feel special and wanted. He had met all her family - a happy little unit of their own. But if he moved in with her he might have to give up the golf - why? He had played golf ever since Silvia was a child. She was banned from watching Top of the Pops because Peter Allis was on the other side narrating the boring sport of grown men in strange trousers hitting a ball around.

He could still afford the membership and he still worked part time as a consultant despite being 70. Or was he worried that he wouldn't be able to keep up the style to which he had become accustomed with Silvia's Mother? She'd always controlled the purse strings and pulled the reigns tight when her Father got too frivolous with their hard earned cash. They never went without but growing up after World War II you learned to count every penny.

It might just be the shock treatment needed to kill off a new romance – the hard facts of life without the rose tinted specs. When someone pays you a bit more attention than you get at home you are bound to be flattered. The old "my wife doesn't understand me" bit has fooled mistresses for years. It's no longer the bartender that listens to the disgruntled husband out for a few beers on his own - other women do too.

So was this it? The marriage breaker. Divorce, sell the house and he goes off to a life of joy and leaves a lonely old lady behind. Roger and Kiki syndrome. Single next door neighbour/friend befriends wife and husband, then she falls ill and husband falls for the damsel in distress because he feels needed and wanted and able to provide, just like when the man went out to hunt and provide food for his family.

Was this some kind of Neanderthal memory bank kicking in that told him this was the right thing to do? She'd won by the sympathy vote. The lonely widow, never able to love her husband again after he did the dirty on her, and here she was now doing exactly the same thing, to someone else. Knowing how it had made her feel she still proceeded with taking a bite of forbidden fruit, the serpent offering an apple to Adam and him taking a bite of carnal knowledge not content with his lot in life.

Silvia remembered an ex of her brother's, who was impressed by the large amount of tax-free lump sum he would receive once retired and made a beeline for him. He was invited to a work ceremony for never having a day off and was rewarded with £200, which she duly snatched from him and bought herself a designer handbag. His name was entered into a draw for a car and the first thing she said was that they could sell it to pay for ballet lessons for one of her kids!

She had her own house but rented it out and was renting a smaller place so he moved in with her. They got engaged that Christmas after she insisted (what is wrong with men?) and then started looking for a place of their own. Of course he used his tax-free lump sum as the deposit on a house, but once installed in the newly refurbished home, the cracks started show after she drank too much wine and started arguing. Silvia could see a pattern developing. It ended one night after he walked out, not being able to put up with the unreasonable behaviour anymore.

The Mad Woman immediately got a solicitor to stop any sale of the house, refused to pay any rent, only the gas, electric and water bills plus the council Tax and demanded 40% of the equity in the house - £35k - all because they were engaged as it's still a legal promise to marry. It took two years to get her out and the money paid her debts off despite getting rent from her own property.

"Bloody gold digger?" Silvia seethed, "it's amazing how some women will do anything to get their hands on other people's hard earned cash".

Silvia was not about to let that happen to her Mother and see her out on the streets at 70 years of age. Silvia would fight and her Father knew it. She was torn, she wanted her Father to be happy but not at the expense of her Mother being alone and homeless at 70 and desperately unhappy. He explained how he was planning to stay in the house but come and go as he pleased and informed Silvia that her Mother was happy for him to do so. Silvia didn't believe it for a minute – what sane woman would let a man come and go as he pleased? It would break her heart, if she had one.

It had taken all his courage to drive the 50 mins journey that had actually taken him 2 hours to arrive (he'd obviously used the time to pop in to see the other one on the way) and tell Silvia to her face. Wracked with guilt and relief that she was still speaking to him, he left in tears to begin the journey back to his living hell.

"It will only take him an hour to get home now," she thought, "and then maybe him and mum can talk some more - probably more than they have talked in a long while and try to sort it all out."

Silvia phoned her Mother - and that's when it hit her. Her Mother sounded calm and a little upset but said she wasn't eating. She said she couldn't stop shaking and retching.

"It was just the shock," Silvia advised her, "I'll take tomorrow off and come over to see you."

"No, no, I'm alright."

"No you're not. I'm coming anyway." Silvia was no "yes" man.

Then she phoned her brother. Neither wanted to take sides but felt more sorry for mum as she was now the lonely one, a very old and lonely one.

Silvia remembered back to when she'd been chucked by boyfriends she'd still loved. The pain feeling as though she'd had a knife thrust through her heart and then someone twisting it. Not being able to eat anything for days her stomach so knotted and tense with nerves and wondering how she was going to cope. But she did and there were many more boyfriends afterwards. She knew exactly what her Mother was going through. Her Mother, however had never been very sympathetic because she had never really understood what Silvia had gone through herself - it had never happened to her before - she had known dad since she was sixteen.

The anger was starting to rise in her chest. Why this? Why now? Maybe they didn't have much time left. You only get one chance to live so make the most of it. Silvia couldn't sleep, she cried till her eyes stung and the lids puffed up like the inner tubes on a bicycle. "Bugger," she said, "what a palaver."

She recalled all the things he'd said. His friend was learning Spanish - are they planning to go off to Spain together? His friend was planning to do a degree in English. All her kids have degrees - how nice, how bloody nice - was this another dig at Silvia because she didn't have a bastard degree? His friend used to have a good job, his friend's done this, been there, done that, tried the pie, got the t-shirt.

But he never went home - he went straight into her arms - selfish git! Silvia never thought she'd be the maladjusted child of divorced parents - at the age of 45!

I haven't slept
I cannot eat
the tears are falling
round my feet

My family split
my love is shaken
all these awful
feelings awaken

My Life is changing
not for the better
I wish my dad
had never met her

My mood is sullen
my throat is choking
today again
my heart was broken

A few months after the breakup, Silvia's Mother said she wished she had a friend she could go on holiday with. Exasperated, Silvia said in her head to herself, "you had someone, dad, and you wouldn't go away on holiday with him. Every time he asked you said no. Every time he suggested a break away somewhere because he wanted to live, you weren't interested. You gave up all your friends and now they won't ask you if you want to go with them. You have no hobbies and don't want to mix with other people, so how are you going to achieve that?"

TAKING MUM TO FRANCE

Les Francaises still hated English toilet rolls, they block up the fosse septique. Our thick, padded sheets of bliss giving a soft touch to your delicate nether regions are replaced by thin, limp squares of single thickness that at the nearest hint of moisture disintegrate leaving you wiping your bum with your fingers. It's no wonder they invented the bidet, which the English don't trust except to wash their feet in on holiday. Who wants to risk scalding water shooting up your tubes when all you wanted was paper not colonic irrigation?

Silvia packed up a survival kit for a week in a Normandy gite:
Tea towels
Dishcloth
Scourer
Tea
Coffee
Sweetener
Salt
Pepper
Plastic cups
Serviettes
3 English toilet rolls
and a bottle of Pimms (for medicinal purposes).

This was going to be a tough week. Silvia hadn't spent that much time in one go with her Mother since she was 17 but she was determined to give her a fun time. A change of scenery might just help her on the way to recovery but Silvia's Mother had decided to have her hair done that morning which would cause a slight delay in departure so Silvia thought she might as well get her own done at the same time. It was getting long and heavy and she'd had to cancel her last appointment due to the flu, and had dyed it herself (suicide blonde – dyed by her own hands) the week after she recovered.
"That should keep me going for a while," she'd smiled as she admired her reflection in the mirror and thought of the money she'd saved.

Now she desperately needed a cut. Luckily it was Friday morning, everyone was at work, the salon was quiet and coiffed her bonce beautifully. She was all set.

After packing the car Silvia set off at noon to travel the 30 miles from Warrington to Wirral to collect her Mother. Her Father had phoned hoping to see if he could catch them all before they left so he could wish them farewell but he hadn't arrived by the time Silvia did at 1pm.

As she packed the car with her Mother's belongings she realised that she was going to need a crowbar to get everything back out again. The boot of the Audi should have been ample for their meagre needs for the week but with a suitcase each stuffed with clothes for every season (Northern France having similar weather to England in September) and an overnight bag for the hotel on route, emergency kit for accidents (as required by French law), camera bag and lenses for those panoramic shots of cathedrals, landing beaches, Allied cemeteries not to mention the 70 metre long Bayeux tapestry, plus the survival kit in a red storage box it was a tight squeeze.

Her Father finally arrived to say a few departing words, issue hugs and wave them off. He was still 'friends' with Silvia's Mother and called in to see her from time to time on his way back from the golf course or when he was sent on a shopping errand for a pint of milk.

Timing was crucial if they were to catch the 7.04pm Eurotunnel train. It was now 1.30pm on a Friday afternoon. They were going to hit Birmingham at 3.00pm and London at 5pm. The two worst possible times, leaving only two hours to get round the M25, over the bridge at Dartford and down the M20 to Folkestone. Silvia dialled into RAC road watch on the mobile for any road works. Should they go motorway or cross-country? English roulette. Silvia decided to zig zag across country to miss any possible delays M53, M56, M6, A50, A14, M11, M25, M20.

They were all hungry and needed a loo stop and a fag stop for her Mother. They pulled into a Little Chef but it was full with a waiting time of 30 minutes. They couldn't spare it so a quick wee and a fag was all they got.

"We'll stop further down," she informed Gorgeous, the designated driver. The next one was empty and suitably refuelled with sustenance they set off on the next leg of the epic journey across country.

On the A14, a fast road the driver had assured her, they hit their first jam. Silvia thought there must have been an accident. Everything slowed to a crawl. Probably rubber-neckers checking out a cheap thrill, but it was only a roundabout and several more followed. "What a stupid idea to put roundabouts in the middle of a dual carriageway!" Silvia said exasperated.

4pm. On past Cambridge and the M11 was clear. 5pm. Another stop for the loo and ciggies. The traffic detector identified several hold ups on the M25 fortunately all going anti-clockwise at the other end of the motorway but with a slow patch straight ahead of them leading to the Queen Elizabeth bridge at Dartford. Crawl, crawl, crawl, four lanes trying to get into two. 6pm – only an hour to go. Chuck your money in the basket and over you go. 7pm, M20 clear.

Of course it was optimistic that they would get half way across the country in 6 hours. Silvia missed the train by 20 minutes and the next one they could get on was the 8.30pm. Half an hour through the tunnel and it was 10pm in France and raining.
"I hope the hotel keeps the rooms," she prayed. An hour to Etaples sur Mer for the overnight stop made it 11pm. They had to stop for directions at a Pizza restaurant (the only thing open in France on a Friday night). Easy peazy lemon squeezy, a mile down the road they found the hotel, booked in and back out again to the pizza restaurant that was now closed. Not much stays open in France past

9.30pm. They found a kiosk open in the town square and sat in the car steaming up the windows with their kebab and chips, washed down with a can of iced tea.

Racing back to the hotel they ordered drinks at the bar and slobbed into cushioned raffia furniture, finally relaxing after an epic 11-hour journey.

Saturday morning. A quick shower and change and a raid of the breakfast buffet table. The sun was shining over the sandy bay and the marina in the distance. Croissants and cheese, fresh baguettes avec confiture, a huge mug of milky aromatic coffee, much to the disgust of the French who prefer to be able to stand up their spoon in their cup. Just the thing to kick start the system. Silvia's Mother's hands were so shaky, she was a bag of nerves, and if you asked for a coffee you got a cappuccino. She had to drink hers with the cup only half full or it would be all over the place.

They checked out of the hotel and set off on the 2nd leg of their tour de France. A slight detour round Le Touquet, a quick peek in estate agents windows, an early morning exchange of Franglais with an eccentric French lady on her way to the market and away they trundled down winding roads through the Pas de Calais countryside to find the A16 motorway to Normandy.

They passed through Berk and other little villages for consideration in their search to purchase a gite for investment and to letting to tourists keen on venturing into France. Of course it would have been easier to get the ferry from Portsmouth to Cherbourg but Gorgeous always turned green at the mention of boats of any kind due to his motion sickness, despite the Travel Caps. Silvia had no problem she'd always had good sea legs in any kind of weather and was once in a force nine gale crossing to Sweden on New Year's Eve.

The cheapest drink on the boat had been Southern Comfort and mixed with lemonade and drank through a straw proved very intoxicating. After collapsing into bed shortly after letting the English New Year in, an hour after the Swedish one, she woke the next day with a head the size of her pillow. In between bouts of sickness she managed to take a shower and get dressed, apply her makeup evenly and venture down to the restaurant for lunch. But it took 5 hours! She thought they were going to die in their cabin and no-one would know where they were until the staff came to clean the room the following day.

So the Eurotunnel was a good option. The journey took them west across northern France with countless stops to crouch over the 'holes in the floor' at motorway service stations, the French call toilettes, passing through 4 regions Nord, Picardy, Haute Normandie and Basse Normandie and 5 departements 62 Pas-de-Calais, 80 Somme, 76 Seine-Maritime, 14 Calvados, and 50 Manche, their final destination. It was 4pm and had been a long drive but they needed to see as much as possible if they were to decide where to buy and to get a feel for a life in France.

Blainville sur mer was a tiny town with a bar that doubled as the bakery and the petrol station. If a car pulled in while you were waiting to be served, the bar tender disappeared outside to fill the tank and reappeared to get you your croissants and vin rouge! It reminded Silvia of the picture house in Hoylake.

A small, privately owned cinema, that struggled to keep open when the bigger competition arrived in Wallasey a few miles away. It hadn't changed in years. It still had the big drapes that opened and closed over the screen and had an usherette selling ice cream in the interval. A bit like the 10 o'clock news interrupting a major blockbuster right at a crucial bit! You bought your ticket and then moved down the line to buy your sweets from the same lady who'd also moved down the counter. Then she'd come round the counter to clip your ticket and show you to your seat. When everyone was seated she go to the projection room and start the film and God help you if the Hoylake Lifeboat went out…

It had been a lovely day weather wise and they'd stopped for lunch in a canal-side creperie in Trouville-sur-mer and watched the world go by for an hour. How very civilized it was too to discover that the French don't charge for parking during the hours of 12 noon till 2pm so they hadn't had to route around for loose change when all they had were crisp new euro notes.

The gite was one of 5 set in the grounds of an old manor house with a swimming pool at the back, all a respectable distance apart for enough privacy, but company if you wanted it. A small orchard was set to the side with a barbeque area. There was a small table and bench outside the front door, pretty enough to sip a glass of wine at and read a book on a balmy evening as the sun set and on which the owner had left them a huge bunch of juicy, green grapes.

They unpacked and set off to find a supermarche for breakfast supplies and find a restaurant for their evening meal. The area was well known for oysters but none of them being fish eaters or slippy slidey thingy eaters, they settled for one with meat on the menu in the next village. Considering the French promote haute cuisine this place sucked. You could resole your shoes with the steak, the pork was tasteless and Silvia found a fly in her meal, but not until she'd almost eaten all of it. She felt her stomach churn and covered her plate with her serviette so the others couldn't see.
"No point in us all feeling sick," she thought.

Off they went back to the gite for Pimms and Whisky, but not in the same glass, and the local speciality cider.

"At least the alcohol will cleanse my stomach of any bacteria the fly may have given me," she mused.

The next morning they awoke to the sound of the toilet overflowing and obtained two sachets of brown powder to throw down it from their host.
"This will unblock the fosse septique by dislodging an airlock and get it running smoothly again," he explained, like the man on the B&Q help desk.

But when Silvia tried to use the shower, the tray turned brown as it backed up through the drains. She jumped onto the ledges at the sides to avoid it touching her feet, in the same way James Bond does when he's in a lift and the floor gives way. She'd read somewhere that you absorb things more easily through the soles of your feet. Not having any bleach Silvia sprayed her Mother's denture cleaner in it and it seemed to do the trick.
"Improvisation is a great thing," grinned Silvia.

"It isn't very French, I know," explained Silvia, after a plateful of bacon and eggs for breakfast, "but the only time I get to have a cooked breakfast is on weekends and holidays. We'll try the baguettes and croissants tomorrow from the petrol station."

Silvia went off to get dressed and returned to find her Mother with a cigarette in her mouth spraying her hair with hair lacquer!
"Yikes mum, are you training to be a flame thrower in the circus?" she yelled.
"What?" asked her mum, completely innocently.
"The hairspray is highly flammable and the cigarette is the ignition, you dummy mummy!"

They piled in the car and set off for Bayeux. The famous tapestry is 230 feet long and 20" high and depicts the invasion of England by

William of Normandy and life in general in XI century. An explanation in Latin is embroidered across the top and for those who didn't read Latin at Oxford or Cambridge there's a translation in English.

Gorgeous was more interested in the patisseries, in which stood great creations made of sweet pastry, apples and cream. He purchased one that resembled the Millennium dome and could have fed a family of 12. It was carried precariously to the car in a huge white box tied with ribbon and placed in the fridge on their return, to be nibbled at for brunch each day with a mug of coffee or a slice with afternoon tea.

They stopped in St. Lo for dinner on their way back from Bayeux but were surprised to find that the whole town was shut on Sunday with the exception of a solitary bar/restaurant that didn't serve food. The next nearest big town was Coutance and it was dark by the time they reached it. They circled round to see if there was any sign of life and saw the warm glow of neon as they drove past an open restaurant opposite the park.

The car swerved into a nearby parking bay and screeched to a halt. There was the sound of three clicks unlocking seatbelts as three doors flew open simultaneously, and six feet ran towards the door. After only a croque Monsieur all day they were faim-ished.

Warm inside on this cool evening they settled down to enjoy a most welcome meal, listening to conversations from other tables - some French, some English - and noticed how loud people talk when they think no one can understand them. The waitress pulled a face that resembled a cat licking piss off a nettle when the next table returned a plate of raw mince to be "bien cuit" after mistaking the steak tartar for a burger. You'd think the French would know by now that the English don't have the stomach for "blue" meat but in France the chef is always right not the customer.

The temperature was dropping and when they reached their gite it was cold inside, too. They plugged in a small heater to take the chill off but every time it reached its thermostatic temperature the lights dimmed as it clicked off. Then, suddenly, they were thrust into darkness. Gorgeous ran to the car for a torch. He had a thing about torches. It happened every now and then. First it was rugs, he kept buying one every time they went shopping and soon the whole house was covered in rugs. In every shape, size and colour. When he started putting them outside the front door, Silvia had had to give him an ultimatum.

"Stop buying rugs or I'll beat you round the head with one," she said.
It seemed to do the trick.

Then it was bags, travel bags, suitcases. Tool boxes, at least 5 all full of rawl plugs of every colour, shape and size. His eyes lit up every time he passed some in the DIY shop, and of course, a girly one for Silvia small enough to keep in the kitchen cupboard so she didn't have to disturb the spiders in the garage to get a screwdriver.
"You see this screwdriver?" Silvia showed him.
"OK I'll stop," he said.

Then came the First Aid kits. One in the kitchen, one in each car boot, one in each of the bedside tables. All full of plasters and bandages of varying sizes and tubes of things for muscle aches, mouth ulcers, cleaning wounds and easing stings and bites. Stuff to rub on your chest and shove up your nose. Eye drops, ear drops and cough medicine. Lint. Tablets for headaches, tummy aches, indigestion and diarrhoea. All out of date and packaging turning yellow with age. You could guarantee that if you wanted anything in an emergency it would be in one of the other ones!

Garden furniture. There was only the two of them but they had acquired two dozen white, plastic chairs with contrasting green cushions, three matching tables with umbrellas but blue and brown ones - don't ask - and long cushions for the garden benches.

Swiss Army knives - including the one which Silvia had used to defend herself against the mugger - and Leatherman tools that you could build a boat with if you were ever marooned on a desert island, and had a million and one other uses that would make McGiver jealous, but they were always being confiscated at customs because he kept forgetting to take them off his keyring when they travelled.

Now it was torches. There was one in every cupboard in every room in the house. In both bedside tables. In both glove compartments. In both car boots emergency packs. In brief cases and handbags, miniature ones on keyrings. In every colour, shape and size.

"Why do we need so many bloody torches?" Silvia shouted, exasperated.
"In case the lights go off when I'm not here," he defended himself.
"Then you'll be able to find your way round the house to fix the fuse.
"The fuse box is in the garage, so it's a pity you didn't buy a miner's lamp that I could strap to my forehead while I used both hands to unlock the four bolts you put on the front door!" The next day he did just that and wore it for bed the next night. As soon as Silvia turned the light out and rolled over to hug him he switched it on and lit up akin to a Christmas tree.

Even his nephew asked his Mother to tell him to stop buying him torches as he'd bought him one every Christmas for the past three years! It cost a fortune for all the batteries and were never used, but left to rust to a gooey mess, lying forgotten for years.
"Gorgeous," Silvia whispered under her breath.
"OK, no more torches."

Gorgeous returned to the gite following what resembled the glare of a passing space ship. Had he captured the full moon and put it behind a magnifying glass? No, it was the biggest torch Silvia had ever seen. It lit up the whole gite with a blue/white glow that you only get with the Colgate ring of confidence.

The owner came out to check they were all right and then his own house was thrust into darkness. He managed to fix the fuse after half an hour of fiddling in a small box nailed to the wall and told them he was going away for a few days. He gave them the phone number of his handy man to ring if they should have any more trouble and replaced the heater with a new one but they were too scared to use it in case the same thing happened and no one came to help. They decided it would be a good idea to go to Monsieur Bricolage, France's answer to B&Q, the next day for some wood for the stove.

Monday morning they went to Granville to visit the childhood home of Christian Dior. They parked the car in the town and walked the winding road up to the house and gardens. The house was now a museum full of gowns worn by royalty and celebrities the world over. The gardens lovingly tendered through which there was an exit that led back to the town via the beach.

It was there that Silvia discovered her Mother's fear of heights. As a child Silvia never knew her Mother feared anything. Whenever Silvia was frightened, her Mother used to say, "Oh don't be stupid, it doesn't hurt." This was her standard reply to Silvia's fear of the dentist, fear of injections and any other fear she discovered as she grew up, spiders, falling off her bike and scraping the skin off her knees, falling in the playground and smashing her teeth on the gravel. Silvia thought her Mother was the bravest person alive.

When she was sixteen she went with her Mother to a fortune-teller and a cat walked in the room. Silvia's Mother froze. Silvia shooed the cat away and her Mother confessed a dislike of them but couldn't explain why. She thought she must have had an encounter with one as a child and the fear had stayed with her.

When Silvia's Mother retired she decided to take a trip of a lifetime to the Far East. She needed lots of injections for Yellow fever, Cholera, and Hepatitis. She mentioned to Silvia that she was worried. Silvia looked at her shocked, "But Mum, you used to drag us kicking and screaming to get our jabs and you told us it never hurt and it was nothing to be afraid of, and it did and it was."
"Yes, but I couldn't show you that I was afraid as well, otherwise you'd never have gone," she answered, matter of factly.

She had a point. It must have pained her to see her kids suffer and not be able to do anything about it. She had put on a brave face and appeared totally calm throughout their hideous ordeals. And here she was now standing on the top of a staircase leading down to the beach about 100 feet up.

Silvia took her arm so she was on the outside and her Mother was on the inside with less of a view and proceeded to lead her down, slowly, very slowly. An old Frenchman appeared behind them, about her Mother's age and nodded in empathy. He mumbled something unintelligible and pointed to his knees. They stopped to let him pass and realised he thought she was having trouble with her knees and that's why she couldn't get down the stairs too well. He hadn't noticed the fear in her eyes at all, he'd mistaken it for pain.

They drove on to Mont St. Michel but once they saw the amount of stairs there it was pointless going any further. They glanced in the few shops at the bottom and decided to go and find Monsieur Bricolage or they would be cold again that night. Unsuccessful, there wasn't one to be found all the way back to the gite so they collected some dried pine cones in the grounds of the manor house and used old newspapers to light a fire. They were snug that night.

The next morning the warm September sun rose steadily into the sky but not high enough to be able to peel off some layers and enjoy it on the skin. It was still warm enough to walk around in without feeling uncomfortably moist, in the same way a damp towel does after your shower. As the summer's humidity dried out it left beautiful, sunny days and cooler nights for restful sleep.

Silvia and Gorgeous descended backwards down the wooden staircase from the mezzanine bedroom into the lounge. Its usual purpose was to transport two very small children up to their beds but the thought of Silvia's Mother trying to climb it at 70 years old filled her with dread. There was no handrail and resembled more of a ladder you'd see on bunk beds. So they gave the only bedroom to her for privacy and diced with death every night as they scaled what resembled K2 after a bottle of Normandy cider.

The bedroom door was still closed and although it was 10am it was unusual for her Mother to still be in bed. She looked at the bathroom door. No that was empty. She walked over to the bedroom and tapped lightly on the door. No answer. Silvia started to worry that something might have happened in the night. Had she fallen asleep with a cigarette in her hand? No, if there was a fire they'd be dead as well. Did she drink too much whisky and fall asleep on her back only to choke on her own vomit. She called out to her.
"Mum!" No answer.
She knocked harder this time. No answer. She turned the handle as panic rose in her chest at what she might find behind the door.

Nothing. The room was empty. Where had she gone? She couldn't speak French and it was Tuesday. Nothing opened in the village on Tuesday. She looked at Gorgeous.

"Don't worry, she can't have gone far," he consoled her.

"Yes, but she might not remember her way back!" Silvia snapped.

She put one leg in her jeans and hopped round the floor whilst trying to tuck her nighty into them while slipping on her shoes at the same time and was about to open the front door when it opened for her.

"MUM! Where've you been?"

"The petrol station to get the baguettes for breakfast," she replied as if it were the most natural thing in the world. "I went to see if I could get my hair done at the Coiffure's but she told me to come back next week. There was no one else in there and I said we wouldn't be here next week. So I walked up to the petrol station to get the baguettes. Why are you trying to tuck your nighty into your jeans?" she asked as she moved toward the kettle.

After breakfast they headed for Coutance and the park they'd seen the night before. Le Jardin des Plantes had over 47,000 plants and rare flowers. It had been illuminated but Silvia considered parks never a place to venture in the dark, so they had decided it would be safer in daylight.

Set over three levels it was the perfect place to sit and relax. A meeting place for the elderly of the town who congregated in the centre around a spiral mound. Gorgeous ran to the top of it and took a photo of Silvia and her Mother from above.

"I'll put it in a frame for you when I get home," he told Silvia. "A little memento of the holiday."

Silvia thought how nice it was to see men and women sitting, chatting together, a sight you rarely saw back home. Everyone stayed in their own gardens and rarely ventured outdoors to mingle with others except to get food, beer, fags and put the lottery on. Then returned to their TVs or computers for their night's entertainment with a spot of Silver Surfing.

They spotted Monsieur Bricolage on their return to Agon for dinner and stocked up on logs, but the restaurant was shut. It was Tuesday. They jumped back in the car and drove back to Coutance. They'd had coffees earlier in the afternoon in a little hotel restaurant they'd discovered as they toured the town on foot. It was an hotel, it had to be open for residents. They were in luck. Silvia was starving and ordered a big, juicy sauccisse. Her Mother ate gammon and egg and Gorgeous had his usual steak.

The next day the sun hit the manor house with a vengeance. A great day to do nothing but lie in it and finish off that Millennium Dome patisserie in the fridge. The apples were beginning to fall from the trees in the orchard and would later be collected by a cooperative to make cider for the region once they had rotted a little. There was no one else about. The other residents appeared to be out which left them sole use of the pool. They went to investigate.

As they opened the gate they saw the pool - covered with a tarpaulin and weighted down round the edges with huge rocks!
"Bloody hell!" Silvia exclaimed. "They covered the bloody thing because they've left town and it's an offence to leave a pool unsupervised. Bugger, the only day we decide to stay here and we can't even use the facilities!"
So they lay their towels on the grass and settled down in the sunshine for a few hours.

They set off for Cherbourg for lunch the following day. A massive town where the ferries come in and unload a stream of traffic. The bustling streets of beeping horns and hazy sunshine proved a bit too much on the nerves so Gorgeous suggested a meander back through the small villages they had passed on the way there. One such village was called Les Pieux, a pretty little place with a small row of shops. Silvia's

Mother spotted a coiffure and decided to go and get her hair done. Silvia followed her in and requested to colour it 'rouge' as a joke.

While she was in there Silvia and Gorgeous decided it was a good chance to mooch around some immobiliers to see how much property was in the area, but no matter what took Silvia's fancy Gorgeous wasn't taken at all with. Silvia fancied a little bolthole that maybe would be something traditional that they could renovate. But Gorgeous wanted something more modern, all singing, all dancing and ready to move into.

"If we are going to rent it out," he explained his thinking, "then we need it ready to move into, as we don't have the time or the inclination to find someone willing to take the project on and get it finished in time." "I suppose you are right," Silvia said wistfully, at the thought of what might have been possible with the time to do it. A romantic, pretty little place, with wooden tables to eat off, and a gingham curtain on the kitchen window.

That night Silvia's Mother had a bad night. The reality of what had happened those few months earlier in April came back to haunt her with a vengeance. Usually by now, 5 months, was ample time to get over a broken heart and be thinking about your next love, in Silvia's eyes, but not Silvia's Mother's - she feared she would never get over it and a daughter and her boyfriend were no replacement for the arms of your husband around you.

Silvia decided they should leave the gite a day earlier than planned and drove through Cote Fluerie coastal villages passing through Deauville the scene of horse racing and the Cinema Americain Festival, Trouville, Villerville and onto Honfleur. It was a busy weekend in Honfleur, it seemed that all the Parisians had come down for the last weekend of summer and all the Brits had parked up on their way back to Blighty. All the hotels were full, and even a motel they spotted on the outskirts of town with their own little patios outside the rooms had COMPLET (no vacancies) on their hoardings.

So they drove around and around and spotted a Chambre d'hote, but that was also full but the nice man was helpful and informed them, "I have a friend who might have a room for you." A phone call was made and directions given and they arrived at a beautiful, architecturally designed house, with paintings for sale for 600 euros adorning the walls.

The owner was the artist and an architect. He had designed the house himself - just like Silvia had wanted to. He showed them to their rooms, they were large and beautifully decorated and inter-connected by a communal bathroom.
"This could be tricky," mused Silvia. "We're going to have to sing very loudly when we are in there and hope mum has her hearing aids in so she doesn't walk in and get a shock from seeing Gorgeous naked in the bath, or I could be getting my inheritance sooner than I think."

They freshened up and set off on foot for the harbour, which picture is featured in all the literature about Honfleur. Although the town was packed the restaurants were still pretty empty, as the French prefer to eat late. They settled themselves in a corner on the inside as it would get cold later on if they sat outside on the pavement. The restaurant retained some of the days heat and was now a comfortable temperature to enjoy their meal. Silvia's Mother ordered the shrimp - she was partial to a prawn cocktail.

Next morning Monsieur le Architect had his housekeeper heat some croissants and baguettes and served them with butter and jam and a large pot of coffee. Silvia tried to chat to him but he was obviously not that interested in any pleasantries she had to offer and he remained aloof. She asked for some information on his house should they ever come back or that they could recommend to their friends and instantly regretted it. He was reluctant but passed her a postcard with some abstract pictures on it making it look a little, happy place that it wasn't. Then gave her the bill. 60 euros a room. It had only cost twice that for the whole week at the gite!

Silvia paid him without question and they departed for Calais, driving across country that was once occupied by German soldiers and Allies in trenches fighting them off, passing through more little villages to Arras's main square and lunch and shopping before stopping off at the duty free supermarket to stock up on cigarettes and 6 bottles of whisky for her Mother. If she could have lifted the shopping basket she would have filled it to the top.

It was a good holiday, and one her Mother had needed badly. A change of scenery does you the world of good.

THE LOW-COMMOTION

Silvia heard a commotion. The creative director was throwing a wobbler over a member of staff leaving early. He'd already phoned the boss to express his disgust.

"He's bloody left early, off skiving again no doubt, and Clara needs a hand she's really busy!" he screamed, until blue in the face.

"He's not skiving off," replied Silvia, "I gave him permission because he finished everything he needed to do and worked through his lunch." There was a stunned silence as he realised he'd waded in without checking his facts first and began an embarrassed babbling.

"But he's so bloody negative about everything you give him that people won't give him their work and everyone else has to do his stuff!" he smirked in the style of Damien from the Omen.

"Yes, he is negative, but no they don't have to stop giving him their work because it should come through me anyway and I give the work out! Silvia shouted back at him. "If that is the case that execs are sneaking in their stuff to the others that I am not aware of and the others do someone else's quota then that buggers up my schedule for the day when I'm trying to meet deadlines. I need them to speak up so we all know what's happening and something can be done about it. How can I control anything if I don't know it's happening? If everything went through the proper channels I would be able to see that everyone is given equal amounts of work to do." Silvia smirked back. "It isn't good trying to sneak it in behind my back as everyone loses out then!"

"If it was anyone else I wouldn't mind," he whimpered, "but he just drags everyone down."

"Then let them complain in their reviews! I can't wipe everyone's arse for them. They're grown people who should learn to fight their own battles or they will get walked over! Anyway, you're the Creative Director – put a stop to it or do something about it. And by the way, **you** could have helped Clara by the time you've taken to complain! And why has she kept all this to herself until now – no bloody forward planning as usual. Too busy organising her social calendar instead I bet.

Another shitty day in paradise. It was always the same, day after day. No matter how hard Silvia tried to schedule the workload through the studio, there was always some sneaky account executive trying to jump the queue, because they thought their work was more important, and Silvia always got the blame. So frustrating, with clients chasing their work and deadlines looming, causing more panic and all unnecessary in Silvia's eyes, but everyone was reluctant to change anything.

Luckily the bank holiday weekend was approaching and she could check out for a few days, to calm back down.

FESTIVAL WEEKEND

Silvia had lived all her life on Merseyside, although where she was born once belonged to Cheshire. Ironically, she'd worked in Manchester almost as long as she had in Liverpool. She felt she no longer knew the place, except at weekends when she'd go shopping in the city. The scouse accents seemed to be more scouse and when Silvia spoke they looked at her as though she was a foreigner, an alien, a Manc!

She'd started using phrases like "Who wants a brew?" instead of "Would you like a cup of tea?" The Mancs called her scouse and the scouse called her a Manc. She was homeless; she felt she didn't belong with either of them.

Silvia felt she knew Manchester more intimately than Liverpool but hardly ventured out there for entertainment. So she decided it was high time she got to know an old friend again when the chance to explore all the places she'd read about in the Liverpool Echo finally arrived, on a glorious Bank Holiday Weekend.

Silvia rounded up a few enthusiastic friends who were game for adventure and off they set, Silva heading west, them heading East to meet in the middle at Victoria monument in Lord Street.

Liverpool was celebrating another year (where had she been all those other years before?) of daytime partying at the Beatle Convention and the Matthew Street Festival.

Every street was closed to traffic and in its place was a bandstand each one playing rock, jazz, blues, you name it, they played it. Every bar was filled to capacity as scousers and homeless scousers crammed themselves in so as not to miss out on the fun. Sardines creating steam heat, squeezing to the bar for refreshment, a quick listen and then off to the next port of call, afraid it will all be over before they've seen anything at all.

They took a right off Castle Street into Mathew Street, home of the Cavern, new bars never ventured, restaurants with French names, culture! Now even more bodies manoeuvrering the narrow backstreet. Radio controlled stewards directing the flow of human lava North and South, up and down, side to side. Laughter, joking, pushing, shoving and then being catapulted to freedom and air.

A quick dash through the city centre and up to Concert Square and an open air cafe - the likes of which she'd never seen on Merseyside and only under cover of canvas in Manchester because of all the rain. If it hadn't been for the wasps she might have relaxed and enjoyed it but there's something sinister about wasps. All you can do is flail your arms around like a windmill to deter them.
"Bees are nice, they buzz your ear and fly away but wasps have developed a quieter buzz, the stealth bomber of nature, so you are less aware until the damn things are in your ear or your drink or up your sleeve! You shoo a bee and it goes away, you shoo a wasp and

he goes off to find his mates then comes back with them," she told her friends.

Abandoning all hope of a peaceful respite it's around the corner into Bold Street, another bar with murals of cupids and naked beings, Gods, angels and an elixir named RED. Named after Liverpool perhaps? Or because the fruit it was squeezed from produced the almost luminous colour of crushed ladybirds. The bottle assured Silvia there were no E-additives enclosed despite its radioactive appearance, so she drank of the cup - she needed all the help she could get.

Uphill now, to the famous Philharmonic Pub, only to find it closed? The most famous pub in Liverpool, closed!
 "Thank heaven for that elixir!" she exclaimed through puffing breath, "I might not have made it otherwise. How can it be closed on the busiest day of the year? Doesn't make sense, they'll lose thousands. Sales Prevention Officers again."
Then came the rain, yes, a typical English Bank Holiday weekend.

They all jumped a taxi back to Mathew Street and into the French restaurant for some culture. A fine cuisine at a fine price and ready to face the music again they descended onto the street once more. A huge roar of thunder and a flash of lightening forked overhead. A cheer went up from the crowd as if in agreement with nature that Liverpool was electric, the atmosphere was electric, this was it, this was where she wanted to be, this was home and it was Liverpool.

She needed to look for a job back in Liverpool. She needed to escape Manchester and the frustrating workload/office politics. She needed her life back so she could live it, instead of being knackered and stressed all the time.

"I'll start tomorrow," she said defiantly.

SILVIA'S MOTHER

Silvia's Mother's life continued to be an unhappy one. She didn't mix well with other people anymore and rather than join a club and meet people of her own age, she preferred to sit at home and smoke and stare out of the patio windows without opening them, so the room filled with fog, while she waited for the one thing she craved, for dad to come back home.

"Is it out of shyness?" Silvia asked herself. "She never used to be shy - the life and soul of the party her friends used to say, but she doesn't have friends anymore. She chose to lose contact with them so she could spend all her time with dad, but he left when her drinking became too much and she'd have a go at him over nothing."

"Fear perhaps? She was brave enough to have her ears pierced and pass her driving test at 50, have her cataracts removed and undergo a partial removal of her colon to cancer, but never bothered having the grommet operation that would prevent her profound deafness and enhance her life. Now she was isolated and lonely in her own little world not hearing conversations so unable to join in - or unwilling to join in - even with the help of two hearing aids."

"Whoever invented these tiny machines obviously never wore one themselves or they would realise the design fault," Silvia pondered. "Maybe they never noticed that the ear canals are at the side of the head but the microphones on hearing aids are at the back of them, so all Silvia's Mother could hear were conversations of those behind her but not in front of her! Pointless, but she'd make a great eavesdropper or spy. Why didn't they put the microphones at the side facing outwards to replicate the ear canals? Wearers would be able to use their telephones in the normal manner and place the earpiece to their ear rather than trying to hold it at the back of their head where the mic is but with the mouthpiece too far away from their mouths so the caller cannot hear them properly either!" So bloody frustrating, she muttered to herself.
"How many deaf/hearing loss sufferers are there in the UK? How many suffer in silence? How many could benefit from this? So frustrating," she announced.

Silvia resorted to buying her Mother new telephones with a hands free button so she could hear people as though they were in the same room but then everyone else could hear the conversation as well. Not very private! Patent pending - one hearing aid with microphones on the sides of them so people can hear near to normality again. Or even better have the microphone at the front of the hearing aid so you can at least hear the people you are facing and not eavesdropping on the scandalous tales being told behind you.

Silvia investigated alternatives that might help, only to discover that you need various other accoutrements to carry around with you. "How ridiculous it is that to get rid of all the background noise you need another machine that you carry around with you for noisy places like restaurants that you plonk on the table, more expense, more inconvenience, not suitable for all, causes embarrassment for people, or you have to wear a contraption around your neck like a stethoscope. You need a bigger handbag to carry all these weighty items around with you and most of the people who need this stuff are frail old people - no wonder they can't walk very fast if they are carrying an extra stone of equipment around with them!" she discussed, exasperated.

So Silvia's Mother preferred to switch off her hearing aid when the child behind her screamed, because she can hear that alright and her head disappears down her blouse with the shock thus missing out on the conversation that's taking place in front of her, once again feeling isolated.

A NEW LIFE

Silvia ordered the Liverpool Echo and began her search for a new job and a new life back where she felt she belonged. Work was changing and new technical people were beginning to fill the building, investors and board members taking up any free office space they could. Lobbyists of all things and Silvia wasn't quite sure why, until the announcement came that they were going to buy up and take over any small business they could that would make them the biggest in Europe.

The boss stepped down to concentrate on other ventures and announced his replacement, Richard Head, or Dick for short, who'd only been there five minutes and had come with a string of clients and promises of grandeur, which won him the position. Within weeks his clients had all left, and all the production work had dropped off.

Most of the staff could see right through him, but played along. He was an embarrassing character not unlike David Brent and gave Silvia tasks he thought she wouldn't be able to handle or solve. She did. Silvia knew he was playing her, because these tasks that weren't part of her job description. He wanted the reception floor replaced and asked Silvia to sort it. So she played him at his own game.

Silvia's Father, unbeknown to Dick, worked in the flooring industry, so she asked him to come in and measure up and provide recommendations. Silvia wrote the report he needed to proceed, which required the removal of the old floor and the reception desk clearing, the closing of the building overnight so they could work on it fume free from the screed needed to level the floor, and the new tiles laying, but he never did. So she knew it was all a game and didn't want to give him an excuse to sack her. She knew people in the business that knew him and the games he played, too. They all said the same thing, "watch him".

When Silvia arrived at work one Monday morning, she stepped through the door and tripped.
"What the fuck!" Silvia exclaimed.
There was a new floor, but it had been laid over the old one, raising the floor level by an inch. People coming out of the lift tripped, staff coming out of the back office tripped. Silvia was instructed to print sticky back notices for all the doors to warn people of the trip hazard. Dick's idea of health and safety.
"Fucking idiot," she fumed.

A few months later the inevitable started to happen. Dick looked into each department and began to weed out the people he didn't like, regardless of them being experts at their trade.

At the end of a particularly horrible week Silvia arrived in work and sat at her desk opposite Ponsonby Smythe. He held up a long white envelope and Silvia asked what it was with a puzzled look on her face but intrigued.
"My resignation," he said.

Silvia was shocked, she'd worked with him for years and although there were times when they argued and fought, they had kept each other's head above water in the bad times and he'd taught her a lot about production and print. She owed most of her experience and knowledge to him.
"I'm going before I'm pushed, because it's going to happen, you only have to look at what's going on around here," he told her, "and I'm leaving tonight."

Ponsonby Smythe was proved right. The first to go was the techno guy's leader, he literally disappeared overnight, no warning and no notice. Then he started on the PR department.

Silvia arrived at work and went to open the door, just as a PR junior brushed passed her, crying, on her way out.
"What's wrong with her?" she asked the receptionist, a scruffy looking tart, who always looked like she needed a good wash. She had only worked there five minutes herself and had started a relationship with another staff member, despite them both living with other people and had broken up his relationship but had somehow managed to keep hers in tact.
"She's just been made redundant," she smirked, with no compassion whatsoever, "and Dick wants to see you as soon as you come in."

A feeling of excitement rose in Silvia's chest.

"This is it," she thought to herself, with a poker face, not wanting the receptionist to read anything into her expression, "my turn now is it?"

She went up to her desk and took off her coat and went to his office. As she entered the top floor, 4 of them were ushered into the boardroom.

Dick had some moral support from the PR manager to make it official.

"I need to make redundancies," he informed them all. "As you know the work has dropped off so we no longer need a production manager, two copywriters and a creative."

"That's because you've lost all of our clients, you dick by name dick by nature," Silvia thought to herself. "Again, I've been left at the mercy of others bad decisions."

"So I'm giving you two days to give me one good reason why I should keep you on," he went on.

"More games," thought Silvia and looked about her.

She could see the others were physically upset. One copywriter was older than Silvia and she knew how talented he was but would struggle to find another job that nurtured him like a family member, as their team had done. The younger copywriter had just got married, had a baby and bought a new house.

"What a twat," thought Silvia, "he's picked the vulnerable."

Silvia spoke out loud and clear, "No, just tell me what my package is worth," she demanded.

He was taken aback. He thought they'd grovel and beg and Silvia thought she saw the PR Manager smile, she'd got one over on him, she wasn't going to beg and this could give her the push she needed to get a new life.

"Well I can only give you what the government are offering as standard," he answered.

It was a pittance for all the years of hard work, and she knew he could have paid her from the company but chose not to.
Silvia stood up, "At least it will give me some breathing space," she replied, "I'll start packing my things," she said, and offered her hand for a shake. "Nowt like kicking a man when he's down," she finished.
The PR Manager almost broke into a laugh at the look on Dick's face. Silvia had played him and won.

She walked back to her desk and informed the team what had happened.
She went online and signed up with a local recruitment company that specialised in advertising staff. Within a week they had a temporary job lined up for her in one of the companies the investors had taken over. Silvia considered what would happen when Dick walked into that company and saw her sitting there again. She would have loved to have seen his face, but she knew she needed to move on so declined it.

Peeve approached her for a private chat.
"I have some irons in the fire," he told her, but I can't tell you what they are yet, but as soon as I know I can offer you something.
"Thanks," she said, "but I need to go it alone, a new start, in a new direction, a new challenge, a better life."

At the end of the month, Silvia received her severance pay which wasn't as much as promised and it had been taxed by mistake."

Only one of the four was kept on and many more followed them over the next few months, and Dick landed himself in court for not following the proper procedures for redundancies. There had been no 3-months official consultation notice with pay. No offering to find another position within the company. It cost the company more than it should have and in the end the board fired him. Karma, what goes around, comes around.

But she was finally free.